THE CERTIFICATION OF AMERICA

THE CERTIFICATION OF AMERICA

The Decline and Restoration of the American Republic, a Fictional Trilogy

VOLUME I

**A Novel By
Paul Seifert**

iUniverse, Inc.
New York Lincoln Shanghai

The Certification of America

The Decline and Restoration of the American Republic, a Fictional Trilogy

iUniverse, Inc.

For information address:
iUniverse, Inc.
2021 Pine Lake Road, Suite 100
Lincoln, NE 68512
www.iuniverse.com

ISBN: 0-595-31498-8

Printed in the United States of America

Author's Note

The Certification of America is the first of three general/science fiction novels concerned with the future of American society. Subsequent volumes of the trilogy will be titled *Dominique Cantrell, First Citizen of America* and *Alexander the Great, 63rd President of the United States.*

The Certification of America is a recipient of the iUniverse **Editor's Choice Award**.

CHAPTER 1

▼

Dr. Jack Salinger stretched like a lazy feline as he crawled out of bed. He yawned deeply, ripped open the lid on a fresh pack of Mary Js, and lit up his first joint of the day.

Toking up with enthusiasm, he sauntered to the refrigeration module and stood swaying at the open door.

Salinger retrieved a prime filet and a package of pre-prepared eggs Benedict. He placed the components of his breakfast in separate microwaves and punched in the appropriate cooking times. He scooped a measure of J. Martinez Jamaican Blue Mountain coffee beans. Salinger pulverized the beans, irritated by the grating whine of the grinder, and placed the grounds in a French press, adding boiling water from the tap.

Noticing that he had not powered down his virtual sex machine the previous evening, he trudged over, still clumsy with sleep, and flipped the switch. The speakers emitted a sexy catcall as the circuitry died.

Salinger returned to the kitchen, retrieved his breakfast, shaved some white truffles over his eggs, depressed the plunger on the press, and poured himself a hefty cup of Blue Jamaican. Then he slumped into a barstool at the counter.

The coffee, brewed strong, assailed his taste buds with pungent flavor. The aroma snaked through his nostrils, jolting him into a higher state of consciousness.

Salinger reached down and ripped a small dressing from his left forearm. Wadding the tape and gauze to a small sphere, he took a dramatic outside shot at the waste receptacle but missed his three-pointer. Compulsively, he left his seat, retrieved the small missile, and dutifully deposited the crumbled bandage into the trash receptacle.

For you, Mother, for you.

In anticipation of his approaching 30th birthday, Salinger had gone to the medical center the previous day for an annual de-fatting infusion. The technician had flipped Salinger's post-treatment scans onto a viewing screen. His arteries were clean.

"Go pig out, Doc. According to the computer, your current life expectancy is approaching 120 years."

Yeah, at least that.

Pig out Salinger did that morning. The savory steak, laced with Hollandaise sauce slightly harsher than he might have preferred, melted on contact with his tongue. He tried to discern the added flavor of the truffles but concluded his taste buds, at least, were approaching middle age.

Salinger checked the time. 8:30 A.M. Too early to log on and open his office.

The scintillating numbers on the LED of the timepiece attested to the very high quality of the grass. Salinger made a mental note to order another carton or two of Mary Js when he placed his next grocery order at We Deliver.com.

Salinger had 90 minutes to kill before his first patient logged on at 10:00 A.M. He picked up his remote and flipped on the floor to ceiling screen of the high definition plasma monitor that covered the north wall of his living space. The sound system always blew him away, especially when he was smoking grass, which was basically every day now.

The thrill of the heavy bass coursed up Salinger's spine like a jackhammer.

He had digitally recorded the *Friday Night Fights* of the previous week. Even if the match went the distance, he had time to watch the first bout. He punched in the numbers. The greater than life size images of the fight announcer and color commentator filled the wall in stunning clarity. Salinger could count the scars and blemishes on the color commentator's rugged face. He could not help chuckling at the so-called boxing expert's relatively high-pitched voice.

Too many low blows.

The joke was inane, but Salinger could not forego a bout of hysterical cannabis induced laughter.

Where did the National Television Network get these guys?

The "Champ" had never been in the ring. He was a professor of boxing history from Emory Virtual University. But on TV, he was always addressed as "Champ," to heighten the dramatic effect of his commentary.

Salinger ate his gourmet breakfast with gusto, as he watched the screen.

"Fucking grass is terrific," he concluded, before tuning in mentally to the recorded telecast.

The hyped up pre-fight promotional material was fairly stale. The champion, Vallero, had survived eight bouts. Four more victories and he could retire to one of the islands and spend the rest of his days basking in the sun. Marveda, the challenger, was a hard luck kid who had grown up on the inner city streets. This kid was no Angel. Marveda was definitely an earthling. Having the fight of his life on national TV was one of the many disasters that had befallen him.

"Well, Champ, this first bout promises to be a real killer," said John Cusack, the announcer, opening the commentary.

"You got that right, John, these little bantam weights always put on a show."

"Marveda has his work cut out for him tonight, wouldn't you say? What does he have to do to survive this contest?"

"He's got to keep off the ropes, John. If he lets Vallero pin him against the ropes or tie him up in the corners, we're gonna see a quick victory for the champion."

"So how does he do that, Champ?"

"He's got to use any quickness he can muster, John, and he's got to dance and jab all night. He has to do anything he can to keep off those ropes."

The first couple of rounds were dull, but then the pace of the bout picked up in the closing seconds of the fifth round. The challenger Marveda scored a hard left hook that staggered the champion momentarily.

Blood was flowing freely from the faces of both fighters.

Salinger was on his feet, sparring and shadowboxing, first imitating the moves of Vallero, then the challenger. Sweat began to pour down his face.

"What a bunch of pussies those guys must have been in the days when they wore gloves in the ring!" he said aloud.

Suddenly, Salinger saw an image of his brother, Martin, flabby, breathing hard, and wallowing from side to side in front of him, flailing away with ineffective punches. Martin was throwing wild haymakers that fell wide of the mark. Salinger zeroed in, smashing Martin's face with a series of straight rights that buckled his older brother's legs. Martin dropped to his knees and then fell thunderously to the canvas.

"Take that, you miserable bastard," Salinger taunted.

"Marveda has been doing a great job using his jab," the Champ suggested. "For a guy who has never fought in the ring before, he has surprising boxing skills. He's been able to keep the champion from tying him up, John, and what we're seeing right now is exactly what happens when a boxer is able to do that."

"Looks like the champion may be saved by the bell."

"He's lucky, John, no doubt about that."

After the flurry in the fifth round, however, the rest of the fight was uninspiring. Vallero recovered and the two fighters sparred rather listlessly through the later rounds. Marveda had not been given time to train for the fight. He looked exhausted as the bout passed the halfway point. Salinger could sense the lack of enthusiasm in John Cusack's voice, as the final rounds wore on. He stopped shadow boxing and sat back down to finish his coffee.

Finally, the bout was over and the exciting parts, the decision and the aftermath, were on deck.

Vallero won the match by a close split decision. He and his entourage retired to the viewing box. The color commentator interviewed the victorious fighter briefly.

"Looked like he surprised you in the fifth round, Hector. How were you able to recover?"

"I had to call on all of my inner strength to pull this one out, Champ," Vallero commented drily.

"Yeah, yeah, cut the bullshit," Salinger spat at the screen "Get on with the show."

The crowd was standing and beginning the now famous blood chant, as Marveda, the defeated combatant, cowered in the center of the ring. Salinger could sense his own heart rate beginning to rise. He loved these modern fights.

"Look at that poor bastard," Salinger said aloud, as the camera zoomed in for a close-up of the terror-stricken fighter's face, which now filled one entire wall of Salinger's living space.

Four additional referees entered the ring and began to prep Marveda. A rack was lowered from the ceiling and the loser was bound hand and foot in a spread eagle, but upright, position before the cameramen. The crowd was wild with enthusiasm. All of the observers were chanting at the top of their lungs. As a physician and former anatomy student, Salinger appreciated the skillful technique used during the flaying. As the referees slid their hands into the incisions and separated the epidermis from the underlying musculature, Marveda's skin came off in three huge sheets. The agonizing screams of the victim, until the endorphins kicked in, were thrilling to hear. The crowd responded raucously as the round announcer girls stripped seductively, smeared their faces, breasts, and bellies with blood, and then danced erotically around Marveda's still twitching body. Salinger reached down and massaged a growing erection. Then Marveda was given the coup de grace.

Salinger read the slowly scrolling script on the screen that described Marveda's background and the accusations against him. Justice was now swift in America. There were no longer any unnecessary expenditures on long-term imprisonment and no futile attempts at "rehabilitation." The old jury system of twelve honest peers had been replaced by equal opportunity. Any earthling perpetrating an act of violence against an Angel had his or her chance at twelve wins in the ring and freedom, or the privilege of bothering society no more.

Marveda knew better than try to rip off an Angel, let alone assault one, Salinger reflected, as he ambled over to his computer and powered up the holographic imaging module. Marveda had managed to bypass the security system—he was obviously a very smart kid—and make his way through the no trespass zone on the 23rd and 24th floors of his housing unit. He had broken into the living space of an Angel on the 29th floor. Marveda had actually struck the Angel in the face, before the Angel's life partner had downed the intruder with a stun gun.

Despite the heinous nature of his crime, Marveda had been given his chance to redeem himself. He had had a good chance to win his match and almost did in that exciting fifth round. Twelve victories and he could have been out of the system, retired to one of the islands. If an offending earthling couldn't hack it and got beat first time out, too bad for him. The penalties for crimes by earthlings against earthlings offered no possibility of redemption at all.

The crowds—Angels watching the bouts from home and privileged earthlings in the arena—went wild for the fights these days.

Jack Salinger, M.D. took a couple of deep tokes off his Mary J, logged on to his office web site, and went to work.

CHAPTER 2

▼

Salinger brought up his office home page.

His logo was plain and to the point. Suspended in virtual space in vibrant colors, Salinger was pleased with the effect.

"Jack Salinger, M.D., Psychiatrist, certified by the American Board of Psychiatry. On-line consultations and pharmaceuticals."

He had eight patients scheduled throughout the morning and another couple of dozen requests for prescriptions.

He ran the script requests quickly, making sure the data for electronic cash transfer had been transcribed correctly. Then he touched the link to his first patient. Since this was a new encounter, Salinger scanned a questionnaire the individual had uploaded and again made certain the payment procedure had been entered properly.

Salinger activated the audiovisual feed, bringing the patient's image into virtual reality. The crystal clear holographic image was that of a portly middle-aged male lounging in a flamboyant blue and gold silk robe, smoking from an ornate Middle Eastern hookah. He reminded Salinger of a cross between Buddha and the caterpillar from *Alice in Wonderland*.

Looking at his patient, Salinger unconsciously reached down and ran his hands over the ripples of his own six-pack abdominal muscles.

"Hi, Dr. Salinger," the patient said at the prompt. "I see you don't permit visual reciprocation."

From the beginning of his practice, Jack Salinger had decided to use face to face contact with patients only in special circumstances, when he felt the individual had need of empathy. From the patient's perspective, Salinger's image was a sphere suspended in space. The user could select color options according to preference.

"That's right, Mr. Reese," Salinger responded, glancing quickly at the name. "How can I help you this morning?"

"Is this connection secure?" Reese asked.

"Absolutely," Salinger said. "You're connected to a completely encrypted web site, Mr. Reese. Discuss anything you wish. I understand from your questionnaire you're feeling depressed. Right?"

"I don't know if I'm depressed or just totally pissed off," Reese responded.

"What seems to be the problem?" Salinger asked.

"I just can't reconcile myself to the new inheritance laws," Reese explained. "My older sister is an absolute bitch. Since she got her hands on our governor's money, she's been cutting my allowance, because I'm too profligate! I know she'll eventually cut me off without a cent. I've been thinking about some very primitive solutions to my problem, Dr. Salinger."

"Are you suicidal?" Salinger asked.

"Hell no!" Reese said. "I'm thinking that if I didn't have an elder sister, I'd be able to inherit the family estate myself. I have to do something before the little charmer gets herself in trouble and begets an heir of her own."

Salinger scrutinized Reese's face. He looked like he was very serious.

Jack Salinger could empathize with Reese's concerns. Salinger was a second son himself. Because of the law of primogeniture, the Salinger family estate would go to his elder brother, Martin. Fortunately, Salinger's father had made arrangements to protect the interests of his youngest son. Apparently, Reese's governor had not thought highly enough of him to have done the same.

"I assume you've talked to your sister about this, Mr. Reese."

"Of course I have, but the little harlot knows she's got me by the balls."

Salinger thought about the techniques available to modern criminologists.

"You know you could never get away with the murder of an Angel," he suggested.

"Which is exactly why I'm so pissed off," Reese admitted.

"Keeping the estates of Angel families intact is not a bad idea. Think of the economic chaos otherwise," Salinger said.

"Hey, I don't mind the entailment part of the inheritance process," Reese said. "I *want* our money and property to stay in the family. The primogeniture part is what galls me. My sister has her hands on the purse strings and there is nothing I can do to protect my interests. You know when the issue is money, most Angels would screw their own grandmothers—to say nothing of their brothers."

"But primogeniture goes hand in hand with entailment," Salinger suggested. "You know that as well as I do. I'd advise you to get some written assurances concerning your financial independence from your sister."

"Fat chance of that," Reese said.

Restoration of the old estate stabilization laws had resulted in many situations like Reese's. Still, Salinger could see the merits of the system. He was more fortunate than Reese. Even though Martin and subsequently his heirs would inherit the family fortune and homestead, Salinger's father had provided an allowance that would maintain Jack's financial independence from his elder brother.

"Your father must have had good reasons for placing all of your family's money in your sister's hands, Mr. Reese," Salinger suggested.

"Low blow, Doctor! You're starting to sound like sister dearest!" Reese said.

"I'd advise you not to do anything rash," Salinger said. "You know the penalty for murder of an Angel, Mr. Reese. I'd hate to see your execution on national television some evening."

"Hung, drawn, and quartered, hey? The same punishment applied in cases of treason against the state," Reese said.

"Exactly," Salinger responded.

"So what do you suggest I do?" Reese asked.

Salinger checked the time. He had to bring Reese's appointment to a close.

"Well, I'd suggest a trial course of Elysium XL. I could prescribe that for you immediately."

"And you think it would help?"

"Absolutely," Salinger responded. "The drug is guaranteed to eliminate any feelings of depression, despair, or anger you might be feeling."

"What about side effects?"

"Other than a pronounced aphrodisiac effect, there are none."

Reese expressed both his approval and his interest in the sexual benefits of Elysium XL.

"Are you in a traditional relationship, or do you use virtual sex exclusively?" Salinger asked.

"I'm still an old bachelor," Reese admitted. "I'm on a machine."

"What model are you using?"

"An Aphrodite 609."

"I'm impressed," Salinger said. "I'm told she's quite a ride. I think you'll find Elysium XL a definite enhancement."

"OK, prescribe some for me."

"Consider that done."

"Thanks very much, Doc," Reese said. He blew an obnoxious kiss at his scanner before signing off.

Salinger touched his pharmaceutical icon and ran the order. The drug would be delivered to Reese's living space within an hour.

Reese can't be doing too poorly, if he's having sex with an Aphrodite 609, Salinger thought.

He knew about the machine, but had never had the opportunity or sufficient cash to try one—despite his generous allowance. Rentals were forbidden, because of lingering fear of sexually transmitted disease. He had heard that even the learner level program on an Aphrodite 609 was exhausting.

Jack Salinger was far more understanding of Reese's plight than he had admitted. He resented his situation as much or more than Reese did, despite his father's generosity.

Jack's father, Professor George Salinger, was one of the creative minds behind the current political system. George Salinger had chosen his youngest son's unchallenging profession. Professor Salinger had also selected a life mate for Jack. Marla LaBaron was a woman with all of the appropriate credentials necessary to enhance the Salinger name. George Salinger had molded Jack's life the way a common potter might shape a lump of clay.

Jack could not forgive himself for allowing his father such latitude. That he had willingly complied with each of the professor's mandates was humiliating.

Salinger left the computer module and ambled over to his exercise area. Jabbing at a touch screen, he brought up his favorite cut from an old acid rock album. With the refrain pounding in his head, Salinger placed his ankles in a restraining bar mounted to the wall and did full body flexion pull-ups until he could no longer breathe.

When he had finally settled down, Salinger returned to the computer. His abdominal wall was on fire. He took another hit from his Mary J. Reluctantly, he reached out and touched the link to his next patient.

CHAPTER 3

▼

Dr. Salinger's list of clients that morning included a couple of claustrophobic Angels. Angels living in the inner cities were housed in hermetically sealed luxury living spaces in the top floors of high-rises. Building on technology developed during the construction of the first generation space stations, Angel living spaces featured individual heating units, bottled water dispensers, and disposable sanitation modules. Electricity was manufactured on-site using advanced solar powered generators. A security zone separated Angel quarters from the tenements occupied by the earthlings living in the lower levels.

Both of the claustrophobic Angels were having trouble adjusting to life in isolation several stories above street level. The problem commonly afflicted Angels not yet bonded to a life mate. Fortunately, the pharmaceutical industry had developed an anxiolytic called Expanding Horizons that invariably alleviated the condition.

A more interesting patient had been a young woman with advanced pyrophobia.

"I know the earthlings are going to torch my building," the patient had lamented after logging on. Her shrewish face betrayed agitation bordering on hysteria.

Salinger tried the standard textbook reassurance protocol.

"You know, of course, that the penalty for arson is death," he said. "You also surely know the evacuation procedures for your sector?"

"What if the helicopters don't get to me in time, or what if the earthlings find a way to block my alarm system?" the patient countered.

"Think how infrequently that happens," Salinger said.

"I don't want to burn to death like someone in hell!" the woman screamed. She leaned closer to her surveillance camera. The tiny homunculus suspended before Salinger was misshapen and distorted by the lens.

Simple psychotherapy was sometimes effective in hysterical cases like this, Salinger had discovered. He flipped on his own video monitor so the patient could see him. Salinger then posed appropriately, adopting the demeanor of a concerned and forbearing physician. Salinger was said to be handsome, with penetrating green eyes. His self-image was not so flattering. Still, he was proud of his skillful use of what the medical profession once had called "bedside manner."

"You know your emergency escape procedures, right?"

"I'm not sure. I haven't been doing my drills lately," the woman said.

"Okay, I understand. When you disconnect, I want you to get out your emergency pack. Make sure you understand how to use the code card that will let you descend through the security zone. Check your body, head, and facial armor and try the suit on for fit. Have you tested your weapon lately?"

"Are you crazy, Dr. Salinger? I could never shoot anybody!"

"You might have to use personal defense during your descent or along the way to your sector's safe house. Do you know where that is? Is your GPS working properly?"

"I can't stand all of this!" the patient cried. "Look at this face. This skin will be charred to ashes and this hair will be burned off. I know I'm going to die with the stench of my own burning hair in my nostrils!"

So much for simple psychotherapy, Salinger thought. He arranged to send the woman a liberal supply of Serenity 400, as a stopgap, until he could arrange hospitalization for inpatient reeducation.

Routine cases suffering from the typical phobias presented few clinical challenges. Salinger was more concerned by the real psychopaths who logged on from time to time. He often had trouble deciding whether the patient was serious or just trying to have a little fun, perhaps out of sheer boredom. Salinger was not above humoring Angels with advanced cases of ennui. He knew the log-on in most such instances was basically a request for drugs. So long as the cash transfer information was correct and payment was pre-approved, Dr. Salinger was content to offer whatever assistance the patient needed, even if that meant becoming a dupe to the patient's creativity.

At noon, Salinger closed the office for lunch and powered down his computer. Then he prepared and wolfed down a steamed North Atlantic lobster, a delicious Caesar salad, and a split of Grand Cru Dom Perignon.

Recalling his advice to the woman with pyrophobia, Salinger checked his own emergency pack after he had eaten. All of the equipment was in good working order. He sauntered over to the wall-to-ceiling window that comprised the outer barrier of his penthouse unit and looked down at the street 46 stories below. He activated the zoom lens on the outside surveillance camera, adjusted the focus on the monitor, and made a visual descent to ground level.

Ubiquitous statues of Plutus mounted on pedestals at the major intersections caught his eye. Plutus, the God of Wealth, was the most important of the pantheon of state supported deities.

Earthlings were scurrying about or standing idly in small groups. Salinger often wondered why earthlings came to the cities. There was little work available. Most of them eked out a living from state subsistence subsidies or by hustling, whoring, or picking up an odd job now and then from the labor recruitment services. Corpse retrieval was available after major epidemics and there was always work to be done on the antiquated sewage system that serviced the tenements. The central heating units in the buildings occupied by earthlings had been deactivated and open fires were prohibited. Without the steady advance in global warming, life in the winter in the northern tier of remaining American cities would have been intolerable.

Salinger monitored the slow progress of a security force as the squad moved cautiously down the center of the street, monitoring the actions of the groups huddled against the sides of the buildings. The convoy edged past the American flag, wafting in a light breeze. The fly was brilliant green and displayed a militant Angel in full flight descending toward a crowd of crouching figures, their left arms raised in defense.

A more appropriate image, Salinger thought, would have been a huge needle with a camel passing through the eye.

Salinger had not been forced to make a descent to the streets since his arrival in the city. He did not relish the idea of mingling with the owners of the taut faces he captured in turn on his monitor.

A helicopter came into view as the aircraft passed overhead in a descent to the heliport atop one of the buildings slightly below Salinger's residential complex. He locked on the chopper with his surveillance scope and tracked the airbus as the craft gently landed. A group of three Angels deplaned and followed an armed escort into the building.

Salinger tapped at the windowpane. In the days prior to Second Independence Day, the glass had not been penetration proof, as it was now. An earlier occupant of Salinger's living space had taken a direct hit to the head, fired by a sniper hiding on the roof of the building the chopper had just landed on.

Salinger unenthusiastically returned to work. His remaining schedule promised yet another uninspiring afternoon. As the effects of the cannabis slowly wore off, his boredom followed like an oozing wall of mud.

One patient tried to convince Salinger she was afflicted with schizophrenia, which she attributed to Heisenberg's uncertainty principle. The woman insisted her ego had fragmented. At times, she felt she was a luminous wave of pure spiritual energy. At other times, she could see herself as nothing more than a collection of abject particles lost in the vast reaches of space.

The amateur cosmologists were always aggravating. The moony advocates of an oscillating universe tried to persuade Salinger there was hope of cyclic resurrection. The more committed downers lamented the probability of an open universe expanding forever toward cold immutable nothingness.

Salinger enjoyed countering by advocating the *Alice in Wonderland* shrinking universe of Hoyle and Narlikar.

"The universe isn't expanding at all," he would insist, tongue-in-cheek. "Instead, everything is shrinking, including you and me. All of the Angels in America will soon be able to dance on the head of a pin."

The only interesting case that afternoon was a potential suicide. The woman had fallen in love with an Angel two quintiles her economic superior. At least here, Salinger felt he could muster some empathy. He was foolishly enamored of a member of his security team, a chopper pilot named Dominique Cantrell. Because of the economic disparity between his and Dominique's family, any liaison between them was forbidden. Salinger's own predicament was similar to that of his patient.

"I understand the male you're involved with is your economic superior," Salinger said.

"That's right."

"Who initiated the exchange?"

"He pursued me, but I went along at first. I was very flattered."

"Have you been having telecommunication sex?"

Modern telecommunication devices permitted tactile contact. The technology had evolved from the classic kiss goodbye to the use of far more sophisticated sensors and probes.

"Yes, almost every night. The stimulation is driving me crazy, Dr. Salinger."

"According to your questionnaire, your partner has proposed a physical meeting."

"Yes, and I want to go to him, more than anything. But the consequences, as you well know, are terrifying. I just can't go on living like this."

Salinger recorded the male Angel's identification data with reluctance. He was required by law to report such cases of sexual harassment to the State Social Protective Services Bureau. He arranged for the female's immediate hospitalization for intensive in-patient psychotherapy.

Salinger was saved from an irritating Angel obsessed by the inevitable death of the Sun when an instant message from We Deliver.com flashed into his holographic space. He was able to convince the patient that he had an emergency and that the visit had to be aborted. He mollified the disappointed patient, who had a great deal more to say about the obliteration of human culture from consciousness, by agreeing to send some free samples of Elysium XL.

Salinger flicked a link to the We Deliver.com web site and reviewed his grocery list. In addition to the usual supplies he replenished weekly, he ordered a few tins of Osetra Russian caviar, an ounce of white truffles, a fresh venison rack, two wheels of Humboldt Fog cheese, and some pate de foie gras. His mother had always advised him not to shop when he was hungry, but when had he ever listened to his mother? He also added two cartons of Mary Js to the order. Salinger reviewed his shopping cart and checked out. The order, with the moderately expensive marijuana, came to 1236 units.

Salinger had just touched the send button and was about to log off when another instant message flashed into the space before his eyes. The sender identified herself as a first quintile Angel. She asked Salinger to authorize an urgent log-on.

Salinger tried to abort the visit. He informed the user that his office was closed for the day, but the patient persisted.

"OK," he agreed finally, "but please try to make this quick. What can I do for you?"

"Oh, for the love of Plutus," Salinger said aloud, after hitting his muting key. The last thing he needed right now was another psychopath.

The patient had insisted upon visual blackout and was using a scrambled audio feed. But the voice, in distorted computer generated tones, emerging from a dark blue sphere suspended in Salinger's holographic space was still forceful.

"Dr. Salinger, this is the President of the United States."

CHAPTER 4

▼

The log-on was coming from a personal computer. There was no special security encryption, no presidential seal, and no request for his own retinal scans. "Madam President" was bogus all right, probably a party girl looking for a week-end supply of Triple Sex. A direct, honest response seemed the best approach.

"Look, Madam President, just tell me what drug you're after and we can get this over fast," Salinger said. "I've already had a dreadful day. I really don't need anymore clowning around."

"I'm sorry to hear things are not going well for you," "MP" responded. "I really wish I could help."

"Then bring this visit to a close," Salinger responded.

"Please run a security scan on my identification icon, Dr. Salinger."

"Of course, Madam President, anything you say," Salinger replied.

Salinger couldn't believe he was playing along with the game, but he brought up his security application and dutifully scanned "MP's" icon.

Jack Salinger sat staring at the sphere suspended within his computer's holographic field. He reached over and fumbled for another Mary J. He lit it, took a long drag, cracked his knuckles a couple of times, and tried to decide what to do next.

The security software was making a third pass over the incoming identification data. Warning alarms that his highest level firewall had been breached were flashing insistently along the edges of the computer's holographic spatial dimensions. Jack Salinger's patient had been identified, using a high-level security loop, as Miranda Lee-Weston, 62nd President of the United States.

Under the revised American constitution, the president was a figurehead, with only a symbolic role in modern politics. Still, Salinger was again awed by the distinction of the office.

"I suspect you may be somewhat surprised, Dr. Salinger," President Lee-Weston suggested.

"I'm LOL, Madam President," Salinger managed.

"A special courier will deliver a package to you tomorrow morning," the president continued. "Inside, you will find a classical 4½ inch CD-ROM disk. I want you to arrange an escort and take the disk to your local branch of the National Museum of Computer History on Tuesday of next week. You should plan to arrive 15 minutes before closing. An operative there has been given your description and will make contact with you. She will take you to a secure location where you will have access to one of the early 21st century personal computers. Please activate the disk and follow the on-screen instructions.

"Your hard drive will be cleared of any reference to my visit to your web site in 10 seconds. Should you choose to contact the Office of Homeland Security concerning this matter, there will be no corroborative evidence to support any statement you might make. But before you do anything rash, Dr. Salinger, please read the disk.

"I sincerely hope you have a much better afternoon."

The holographic imaging space of Salinger's machine dissolved and remained deconstructed for several minutes. Then his computer rebooted. When he brought up his web site, Miranda Lee-Weston's contact with his office had been erased.

CHAPTER 5

▼

On the Monday following Salinger's contact with Miranda Lee-Weston, Kurt Striker, Director of Homeland Security, placed a call to George Salinger. Jack's father was a senior consultant to the Council of Twelve, the single executive, legislative, and judicial body now governing the United States.

"I'm sorry to disturb you, my lord, but my operatives have intercepted a communication that may be of interest to you."

"Go on, Commander Striker."

"Your youngest son has been contacted by President Lee-Weston," Striker said.

"What was the nature of the communication?"

"We're not exactly sure, my lord. The exchange was very brief and was erased before we had time to record all of the data."

"How did Jack handle the situation?"

"He hasn't done anything illegal, at least not yet. Actually, we have no solid information to suggest he responded at all. But considering his history, I thought I should alert you to a potential problem."

"If he is getting himself involved in some form of radical agitation again, I authorize you to do whatever is necessary, Commander, to ensure the welfare of the country. I trust my personal involvement will not influence your actions in any way."

"Of course not, my lord."

"What are your suspicions?"

"For some reason, our Madam President has contacted a fairly large number of board certified psychiatrists. I have no idea what she has in mind."

"How long are we going to put up with this woman's antics, Commander Striker? The council is not at all confident that her activities are as innocuous as you profess them to be. I could secure an order for termination immediately."

"I see no immediate threat from Mrs. Lee-Weston, my lord. But—as I have suggested many times in the past—activities of this nature make it imperative that you support restoration of the full intelligence gathering capabilities of my office. As you know, there have also been increasing surface-to-air missile attacks on our aircraft"

"The council cannot risk repetition of the disruptive effects on Angel society of the excesses of your immediate predecessor, Commander Striker. I believe the council's position in this regard has been made perfectly clear to you. As for the missile attacks, they are nothing but child's play, Commander. The underground resistance may continue making their primitive attempts to intimidate us, but nothing detrimental will come of their efforts."

"Let us hope not, my lord."

"I have assigned an operative to your son," Striker continued. "I trust you concur?"

"Of course. I wish to be fully informed of any developments."

"Without question, my lord."

"Thank you, Commander Striker."

"My lord."

After concluding his call, Kurt Striker remained seated momentarily at his telecommunication module. The honorific, "my lord," stuck in his throat. He reached over and activated holographic images of his two sons. The eldest, John, had died during the domestic coup that had brought the Council of Twelve to power twenty-four years earlier. John Striker had died fighting for his country.

Striker ran his fingertip over the image of his youngest son. Edward had been killed in a hunting accident on the manor of George Salinger five years earlier. Martin, the minister's eldest son, a boorish clod in Striker's estimation, had accompanied Edward into the field. Witnesses—all members of the Salinger security force—had corroborated Martin's story that Edward's death had been accidental, but Striker had never been satisfied that the truth had been uncovered, despite the rigor of the interrogations, which he had conducted himself.

Striker shifted his attention to the holograph of his wife, Anna. He suffered the usual constriction in his chest as he peered at his wife's image. Striker's eyes hardened, as he fought the emotion. Anna had not been able to survive the loss of both of their sons.

Striker regained control. There was no time for petty sentimentality.

Striker scrolled through the Salinger family portfolio. He could hardly contain the hatred he felt for the Salingers, and for all Angels in the top economic quintile of American society—Seraphim, as they presumed to call themselves. Worse, Seraphim who sat on the Council of Twelve—and their closest advisers—now insisted on being addressed with pompous, but empty titles.

My lord and my lady!

Kurt Striker knew he was a born politician and natural leader. The so-called Seraphim had relegated him to defense of the realm, with no possibility that he could rise to the role he felt he had been destined to play in American politics. The Salingers and their ilk would pay dearly for this grievous mistake.

Striker extracted an electronic book from a locked drawer in his desk. The volume contained idealized portraits of the great lawgivers and dictators from the age of classical Greece and Rome, extracted from Plutarch's *Lives of the Noble Grecians and Romans.* Had political prudence not dictated otherwise, Kurt Striker would have decorated the walls of his office with images of these great politicians.

Rule by a single strong individual represented Kurt Striker's political ideal.

Commander Striker thought about the titular President of the United States. He and Madam President had been engaged in a fascinating game for some time now. He found the president's naïve quest for the reinstitution of democracy contemptible.

Democracy has never been a viable system of government, Striker reflected. Democracy is nothing more than empowered envy.

Striker pulled up a holograph of Jack Salinger and sat staring at the image of a man who would never measure up to either of Striker's own lost sons. What bizarre scheme could Madam President have in mind for a weakling like Jack Salinger?

Striker reviewed Salinger's file. The subject had dabbled in liberal politics in undergraduate school, but when threatened with execution, he had collapsed and had gone sniveling home, like a mewling puppy, to be rescued by his father and elder brother. Striker couldn't be certain who held young Dr. Salinger in greater contempt, Striker himself or the esteemed Professor George Salinger.

Striker slid Salinger's image into juxtaposition with those of his own sons, John and Edward. As he studied Salinger's comparatively bloodless face, compassion—but only momentary compassion—flitted briefly through his mind.

CHAPTER 6

▼

The package containing the CD-ROM disk arrived the following morning, as President Lee-Weston had promised. There was also an electronic message, this time bearing the presidential seal.

"Trust is a human virtue sadly lacking in America at the present time, Dr. Salinger. Although I realize this material could be embarrassing were you to share it with certain officials in our Department of Homeland Security, I am willing to take the risk for reasons that will become clear to you when you read the contents of the disk. Signed, Miranda Lee-Weston, President of the United States."

Salinger arranged for an in-town security shuttle and was transported to the Museum of Computer History, located on the 39th floor of an old office building still in commercial use from the 16th floor above ground level. He arrived just before the museum closed, as President Lee-Weston had advised. Salinger swiped his universal identification card at the entrance. The quick pass of the card through the slot paid his admission fee. He then ambled into the display area. The galleries were empty.

As he meandered through the exhibits, Salinger became intrigued by a display of the technological evolution of an old driving unit called a mouse. The cumbersome little units had been necessary for navigation in the years prior to the development of direct tactile interfacing. He examined a few of the equally primitive devices once used to print hard copies of information during the remote paper age. He activated a display showing a time line for the evolution of rates of information exchange and was astounded by the impossibly slow transmission speeds of only four or five decades earlier. Another exhibit of some interest concerned a process called spamming, which flooded individual computers with unwanted electronic mailings, usually sale pitches by various vendors.

Thank Plutus, such crass advertising was no longer legal.

He had been browsing through the various exhibits for five or ten minutes when a young woman approached.

"Dr. Salinger, please come with me," she said.

Salinger followed the woman into the administrative section of the museum and then into what appeared to be a storage area. He was subjected to retinal scans and then taken to a musty out-of-the-way office containing a desk and a vintage turn of the 21st century computer.

"Please rejoin your shuttle crew at the main entrance when you've finished," the woman said. She walked out of the room and closed the door.

Salinger examined the antiquated PC. He had never used one of these old machines before. The tower component was plugged into a power pack with a crude electrical fitting, the kind that had not been used in decades. Salinger powered up the machine. The program opened to a series of miniature icons scattered randomly across the tiny 36" screen of a unit once known as a monitor.

Salinger had to push a few buttons until he was able to identify the CD-ROM player. Finally, a crude mechanical drawer opened that contained a tray the 4½" disk was designed to fit into. The antiquated machinery was irritatingly noisy. Salinger pushed the disk into position. After an interminable wait of several seconds, the screen was finally activated.

Fumbling with the mouse and the keys of the computer's crude keyboard, Salinger managed to follow the steps of an old installation wizard, as prompted by a primitive on-screen menu. The installation seemed to take forever, but finally Salinger was presented with an image that read "Greetings, Dr. Salinger."

He clicked a button labeled "next." He was stunned. An old-fashioned video "slide show" began to run. A series of two-dimensional images sequenced automatically. The history of Salinger's youthful peccadillo, his involvement with a radical group of Angels during his undergraduate years, played out before his eyes. There were telephoto shots of his participation at illegal rallies, candid shots of clandestine meetings between Salinger and Adam Kennedy, the leader of the group of radicals. Then came the final ordeal of Salinger's arrest and incarceration. News clippings, his arrest records, even the digital equivalents of his mug shots slowly passed across the screen.

Because he was a member of the Seraphim subclass, and because his father was a consultant to the Council of Twelve, Salinger's freedom had been bought. Martin had never forgiven him the immense and irreplaceable drain on the family's financial resources. The family came perilously close to losing Seraphim status. Salinger could have faced the ultimate penalty for treason, as had so many of his less fortunate co-conspirators. The National News Service reported that Adam Kennedy had been killed resisting arrest.

Salinger's father and brother had spared no expense in his defense. Even though he was aware that preservation of the family reputation had been the prime motivation, Jack had benefited from the finest legal team in the country. He had been sentenced to one year of intensive reeducation, under the auspices of a personal deprogrammer.

Salinger was astounded to find so much of his personal history on file. He had been assured that the family's reputation had not been damaged by his youthful recklessness. He had also been told his personal criminal record had been purged of any reference to the incident.

For several years, Salinger had not thought about his earlier political indiscretion. The video had opened old wounds. Salinger shuddered, as he recalled the terror of being arrested and then the degrading interview with his father in the library at Haworth Manor.

"You will never do anything to embarrass this family again, Jack. Do you hear me?"

Salinger could see himself sitting with his hands in his lap, fawning and cringing before his father's onslaught.

"All of your life you have been a spineless milquetoast! And you will spend the rest of your life that way. I am going to send you to medical school where you will study psychiatry, a field you should be able to manage without killing anyone."

"But, Father, I don't..."

"Don't you dare argue with me!"

The hatred in George Salinger's voice seared into Jack's psyche like splinters of broken glass.

"Any income generated by your practice will be used to offset the costs of your stupidity to Martin and me. I will—with the greatest reluctance—provide you with an allowance that will permit you to lead a life style appropriate to a member of this family.

"I would be pleased, in fact, if you refused to accept my generosity. You could follow your political persuasions and join some miserable earthling community. But we both know you haven't got the courage to do that. Your interest in reform was a sham, Jack. This entire affair has been symptomatic of your life-long impotence."

George Salinger seemed to be savoring that last word.

"I'm going to find someone suitable to become your life mate," he continued, "even though I will sorely pity the girl. You will be a dutiful son, Jack. And if you ever betray the Salinger name again, I will kill you with my bare hands. Have I made myself clear?"

His abject response stuck in Salinger's throat.

"Yes, Father, I'll do anything you ask."

The program prompted Salinger to continue. He fumbled with the mouse until he was able to click the appropriate button. A grainy video image appeared on the screen. He recognized the empathetic face of Miranda Lee-Weston. The tiny, two-dimensional image began to speak.

"I'm sorry I had to be so blunt in sharing the previous information with you, Dr. Salinger, but your background leads me to believe that you were once sensitive to the injustices that now afflict the United States of America. As a younger man, you were willing to take action to correct these inequities. I am hopeful that you will be willing to be of service to your country again.

"My confederates and I are drafting a document, entitled *The Certification of America*. The text will declare that the policies of the present leadership of our nation are irrational. The document will pronounce the Council of Twelve no longer competent to govern, by reason of insanity. As a diplomate of the American Board of Psychiatry, as the son of one of the supreme intellects of our time, and considering your earlier political persuasions, your signature on the certification would be of great symbolic, but also practical value.

"*The Certification of America* will become the rallying cry of a call to arms for the 2nd American Revolution. If our efforts succeed, your signature will join those of 56 fellow compatriots on a document that will be celebrated forever in the annals of human freedom. The historical significance of your participation will rival that of the signatories of the 1776 *Declaration of Independence*."

The screen image of President Lee-Weston stopped speaking momentarily. Salinger searched the soft lines of her attractive face for something. He could not articulate what it was he was searching for.

After a short pause, the president continued.

"There is an 18th century painting by the French artist, Eugene Delacroix, entitled *Liberty Leading the People*. I see myself in that painting, Dr. Salinger, but I see you there too. I hope you will examine a reproduction of this striking painting very closely. I hope you will join me in my efforts to restore the values of democracy, freedom, and human dignity that America was founded on.

"I realize I am asking a great deal of you, Dr. Salinger. I realize you have many questions. I am sorry that I cannot address those questions now. I want you to think carefully about what I have said. I am placing a great deal of trust in you. I will be in touch with you again soon.

"Now, please step to the other side of the room."

Jack Salinger moved away from the old PC. The disk had been rigged to self-destruct, an antiquated but effective technique. The machine emitted an acrid cloud of smoke as the CD-ROM disintegrated inside the tray of the driver.

Salinger made his way to the lobby of the museum. He knew exactly what he had to do. He was obligated to contact the Department of Homeland Security immediately. He recalled the long dreary sessions he had spent during his tedious reeducation. Jack Salinger knew exactly what was expected of him.

As he left the room, Salinger raked moist fingers through his scalp. He could not expunge the memory of that terrifying day the security forces had broken into his campus living space and placed him under ignoble and demeaning arrest before the eyes of his teachers and his fellow students.

CHAPTER 7

▼

Salinger returned to his living space. The security squad completed their sweep. Left alone, Salinger held both of his hands before his eyes. With clinical detachment he peered at the fine trembling of his fingertips. He logged on to his office site and ordered a supply of Serenity 400.

His mind in turmoil, Salinger paced the floor until the medication arrived by courier an hour later. He fumbled shakily with the controls on the scanning machine before he was able to visualize the contents of the package and transfer the medication to his receiving module. He quaffed down two of the capsules and then sat quietly in the darkness until the drug took effect. He was finally able to think clearly, although the level of his paranoia had not abated.

Salinger conducted a web search. He wanted to learn more about Miranda Lee-Weston, the appointed 62nd President of the United States. As he scrolled the president's web site, Salinger found nothing in Miranda Lee's biography that supported left wing political agitation.

She was from an established New England family. She had attended Smith College and had then graduated at the top of her class at Harvard Virtual Law School, placing second among 26 graduates. She had served as a clerk for a high-ranking member of the Council of Twelve.

Miranda Lee-Weston had been appointed to the presidency by acclamation, twelve votes for the appointment, none against. Her presidency had been unremarkable. She had performed the duties of her office in exemplary fashion. Her portfolio of published writings contained nothing inflammatory.

She had married Harold Weston, shortly before her appointment to the presidency. Weston had served as the United States Ambassador to England, but he had died in a plane crash near the end of the president's first term in office. The couple had had no children.

Based upon her background and her impeccable record of public service, the president's involvement in radical left-wing politics was inexplicable.

Salinger could only conclude that the person posing as Miranda Lee-Weston was a sham. The bizarre proposal to certify the Council of Twelve no longer able to rule the nation by reason of insanity had to be a practical joke.

Salinger concluded the affair was a trap instigated by the Department of Homeland Security, but why should he be the target of a security probe? Of course, Salinger had heard of cases of random entrapment. Perhaps the national defense computer had simply spit out his identification data at random. If that were the case, all he had to do to maintain his security status was report the incident. Any delay could lead to a formal hearing. His past indiscretion might then have an adverse impact. But his record had been unblemished since his youthful mistake. The ominous possibility of a deliberate probe directed specifically at him for probable cause did not seem likely.

Salinger thought about calling his father, or even his brother Martin, for advice. But what recommendation could he expect from them other than immediate notification of the Office of Homeland Security that he was aware of activity of potential harm to the welfare of the state.

Thank Plutus for Serenity 400.

As the drug continued to ease his distress, Salinger began to review the situation with more detachment.

Suppose the entire matter had been part of a random security probe, or even a ludicrous attempted set-up by the Department of Homeland Security. So what? Salinger was beginning to see another viable option. He could simply ignore the episode and refuse to play along. If he was questioned about any of the details, he could vehemently maintain that he had considered the whole incident laughable. He could take the high road and insist he had considered the matter contemptible and not worthy of a response. After all, how could he have been expected to take "Madam President's" outlandish proposal seriously? Any bored, but talented hacker could have fabricated the CD-ROM and constructed a phony identification loop for Miranda Lee-Weston.

Salinger walked into his bathroom and splashed his face with cold water. He peered into the mirror. He could imagine himself an anatomy student again. He peeled the skin from his face and then lifted off the whorls of facial muscle until his own skeleton leered back at him. The reflected image betrayed the shallow emptiness of Salinger's life. The hollow laughter emerging from the death's-head in the glass taunted him.

Salinger returned to his lounge chair, dialed down the lights, and punched in a request for Mozart's *Violin Concerto in G, K 216*. As the almost heart rending beauty of the slow movement washed over his recovering sensibilities, a sudden, unexpected, and jarring thought invaded his mind. Only a handful of earthlings in America would ever hear this music or experience the repose these transcendental notes could offer the troubled mind. A black market that dealt in cultural commodities existed in the earthling community, of course. Mozart's music was not officially prohibited by the state. Primitive devices existed that could play back such music in poor quality audio formats.

The problem was the fact that the state had chosen to deprive earthlings of education. Most of them had no inclination to avail themselves of the consolations of classical music, or the other fine arts. Salinger sat in his chair as the notes penetrated his mind like a warm infusion of transcendent beauty. He was astounded to find tears streaming down his face.

As if the music and the uncomfortable feelings the piece had engendered had become a catalyst opening new vistas of contemplation, Jack Salinger was forced to face an even more disturbing possibility. The compassionate face of Miranda Lee Weston reentered his imagination. Hers was a face bearing a much greater burden of pain and potential suffering than the shallow trappings of her symbolic office could possibly have engendered. He recalled the sadness, but also the intense resolve in the president's eyes. The concept of trust began to beat like a hammer at the core of Jack Salinger's sensibilities. He reluctantly allowed himself to contemplate the possibility—a possibility remote, but as disturbingly piercing as the music of Mozart—that his strange and puzzling encounter with the President of the United States had been authentic.

CHAPTER 8

▼

Kurt Striker took his seat before the video camera in the Office of Homeland Security. The Council of Twelve had requested a teleconference. Striker glared passively as the holographic images of the ministers materialized in virtual space before his eyes. The black robes and wigs struck him as theatrical.

Striker bowed courteously to the assembled dignitaries. From the perspective of the council members, Striker was seated at a witness table.

"Bring us up to date on the president's activities, Commander Striker," the acting chairwoman began.

Striker nodded graciously.

"Her behavior is strange, my lady," he said. "Madam Lee-Weston has made contact with a large group of psychiatrists, but her motives are not yet clear."

"How large was the group, Commander?"

"Well over 50, my lady."

"Is the number significant?"

"Perhaps," Striker responded. "There were 56 signatories to the 1776 *Declaration of Independence*."

The line of faces responded variously. Smiles were interspersed among expressions far more sober.

"It would appear," the chairwoman suggested, "that Madam Lee-Weston is planning a coup of some kind."

"Possibly," Striker agreed, "but we have no proof as yet. The president's communications with the physicians have been extremely brief and Mrs. Lee-Weston has managed to delete them. We have not been able to intercept any of the transmissions."

"How have the psychiatrists responded?"

The question came from Professor George Salinger, Adviser Emeritus to the Council of Twelve.

"There have been no direct electronic responses, my lord. At staggered intervals, however, the physicians have made visits to museums…museums of computer history."

"You suspect she is communicating using outdated technology?"

"It would appear so, my lord. An effective ploy, I might add, one almost impossible to trace."

"I trust you have inspected these museums?"

"Of course, my lord."

"And?"

"We have found little useful information, I'm afraid. Of some interest, however, the hard drives of several of the old computers we inspected have been removed. Residue recovered from several of the CD-ROM players also suggests the president is using self-destructing disks."

"I think we should confront Mrs. Lee-Weston," the chairwoman said.

Striker's eyes moved slowly from face to face.

"I don't think that would be wise, my lady."

"Your reasons, Commander?"

"I see no immediate danger," Striker said. "I think we should give Mrs. Lee-Weston sufficient latitude to incriminate herself and her co-conspirators, if there is indeed a conspiracy.

"I would like to suggest, however, that the restrictions on surveillance and interrogation that were placed upon the Office of Homeland Security at the time of my appointment be removed immediately. As you know, my predecessor enjoyed much greater freedom of action to conduct unimpeded intelligence operations than I do."

The ministers met privately in plenary session. Striker was recalled following the Council's deliberations.

"For the moment, the restrictions on your office will be lifted, Commander Striker," Madam Chairwoman said. "But we must warn you, a great number of Angels were unfairly intimidated by the tactics used by your predecessor. You must use considerable discretion, Commander Striker. There has been no indication of subversive activity by the Angels of America in over eight years.

"In regard to the president, we advise you to take no immediate action. We expect you to use whatever intelligence gathering methods you feel are appropriate. You will, of course, keep us fully informed."

Striker nodded obsequiously.

George Salinger insisted on a private conversation with Kurt Striker following the plenary session with the council.

"What response has my son made to the president's transmission?"

"Your son, like the others, seems to have developed a sudden interest in computer history, my lord," Striker said.

George Salinger said nothing. His expressionless image slowly deconstructed before Kurt Striker's eyes.

Kurt Striker rose from his seat. Standing before the window, he scrutinized patches of wispy clouds racing across a wind swept sky. He was engrossed by the problem presented by the President of the United States and her cadre of psychiatrists.

Mrs. Lee-Weston had changed radically following the assassination of her late husband, Ambassador Weston. The Weston affair had been Striker's first covert action upon assuming office. Obviously, the president had decided to carry on Harold Weston's fatuous dream of reestablishing democracy in America.

Striker knew he could easily convince the council that Mrs. Lee-Weston represented a "clear and present danger," to use an old expression. The president could easily be eliminated at any time. But the council had finally taken the first essential step toward full empowerment of the Department of Homeland Security. Much more authority would have to be delegated to his department before Striker would be ready to proceed with his own plans. The rope he had advised the council to give the president would have to entangle a few more necks than Madam Lee-Weston's before the council played completely into his hands.

Striker thought of George Salinger with particular distaste. The professor was a pompous, overbearing fool. But his son was a likely candidate for recruitment as a potentially useful double agent. Striker had assigned his best operative to Jack Salinger.

The Director of Homeland Security peered at the somber face reflected in the window. A smile slowly softened the harshness of Kurt Striker's image.

So let the games begin.

CHAPTER 9

▼

Nora Salinger had planned a gala party to celebrate the 30th birthday of her youngest—and secretly favorite—son. The festivities would take place the coming weekend. Salinger managed to close his office early on Friday. He informed his security service that he needed a pick-up for 3:00 P.M.

Responding to the chime in the foyer of his living space, Salinger reviewed the images on the security monitors sweeping the corridor outside. He ran retinal scans on the two uniformed personnel standing in the hallway. The squad in turn reviewed Salinger's own retinal scans. The security software authorized entry into the decontamination zone.

"What level health alert are you reporting?" Salinger asked the squadron commander.

"Level green," the commander said, "Clear for free unprotected access."

Salinger ran a validation check through the Centers for Disease Control. Status green for his sector was confirmed. Ultraviolet, ultrasonic, and low level nuclear decontamination of the security squad would not be necessary.

The earthling sector was constantly monitored for DNA evidence of microbiological contamination. Any evidence that a hot zone had developed was immediately reported and the level of health alert was upgraded to red. In the past six months, level red alerts for two previously unidentified viruses had necessitated full protective gear for all Angels during egress from quarters. Salinger, like all members of his class, had been vaccinated against all known human pathogens. He had been issued prophylactic antibiotics three times during the last quarter. The protective gear was overkill in a few of the cases, but the authorities preferred to take no chances.

Health care for earthlings was basic. In order to maintain the efficiency of the work force, the state authorized selective vaccination for earthlings, but restricted antibiotic therapy to rapidly spreading infectious diseases that endangered Angels. Valuable resources were not wasted treating diseases in the earthling sectors that were of significance to earthlings alone.

Salinger authorized entry into his living space. The two Angels made the mandatory, but fortunately cursory inspection of the residence. The squad commander collected a vacuum filtered specimen taken from the air and furniture in each of the four rooms. The material would be processed at the security base for skin scale DNA. Evidence that any unauthorized individual had entered the living space would trigger an emergency security alert.

After securing the quarters, Dr. Salinger accompanied his escort to the heliport on the roof of the building. He was glad protective clothing would not be necessary in the relatively confined space aboard the aircraft.

"I noticed you had a Venus de Milo back there, Doc," one of the men commented. "How do you like her?"

"She's OK," Salinger admitted, "but one of my recent patients has been using an Aphrodite 609. I must admit, I was jealous…"

"An Aphrodite 609!" the squad commander said, with a whistle. "Now there's a machine I'd love to spend a weekend with some time. Ever tried one, Doc?"

"Nah," Salinger said. "I asked my father to spring the cash for one when they came on line, but he told me I'd have to save up the necessary units myself. You know how it is when our patriarchs get too old for the machines. No sympathy for those of us who are still users."

"Yeah, my governor's like that too."

The group reached the roof through the security elevator. The three men emerged into the muted sunlight and proceeded to the awaiting turbo chopper.

"Who's flying?" Salinger asked.

"Your favorite pilot, Major Cantrell."

"Terrific," Salinger said, with a hint of regret.

"Now that's one sweet little Angel I wouldn't mind spending a weekend with either," the commander admitted. "I'm sure she could run circles around an Aphrodite 609. Too bad liaisons are restricted, hey Doc?"

"Yeah," Salinger agreed, "Too bad."

Reaching the chopper, the three men prepared to board, after donning flight helmets.

"Come on up here with me, Doc," Major Cantrell insisted.

Major Dominique Cantrell was indeed a knockout. Salinger had once logged on to a site that had created a computer enhanced image of the ideal human female, extrapolating elements from the most striking features of America's most beautiful women. Dominique Cantrell's face was a mirror image of that computer-generated portrait. As Salinger surveyed the curves visible beneath the tightly fitting flight suit Major Cantrell was wearing, he sensed a qualm of frustrated desire. He suspected Dominique's body was also a clone of the perfect female form the computer had created.

Since he had met Dominique, Salinger had surfed photography and virtual art collection sites for a face similar to hers. He felt he had come closest with the striking photograph of a mid 21st century Afro-American actress.

Jack Salinger *did* regret the restrictions on physical contact between members of the five economic subclasses of Angels. He regretted those restrictions very much.

Twenty-four years earlier, when the plutocracy had been established as the official government of the country, the ruling class had been designated Angels. Under the new constitution, the monied class had been divided into five quintiles—economic subclasses based upon graded wealth as existed on Second Independence Day. All executive, legislative, and judicial functions were now the prerogative of a single administrative body, the Council of Twelve. Only members of the highest quintile—Angels referred to as Seraphim—were eligible to serve as ministers.

Although movement from one economic subclass to another was theoretically possible, a national program of wealth maintenance made such events extremely rare.

In order to stabilize the situation further, iron clad laws on inheritance, entailment, and restrictions on interactions between the five economic subclasses of Angels had been established. Any infringement by an Angel of any subclass on the existing order was considered treason against the state, punishable by the ultimate sacrifice of the perpetrator and, in some cases, the offending Angel's immediate family. The executions of convicted Angels were broadcast on national television, in conjunction with the public sporting events involving earthlings guilty of crimes against Angels.

As he climbed into the seat beside his comely chopper pilot, Jack Salinger regretted that he was a Seraphim and that Dominique Cantrell was four quintiles below him on the economic scale. Any intimacy between them was strictly forbidden.

"Hi Doc," Dominique said with a searing smile, as Salinger strapped himself in, "How are things with my favorite psychotherapist?"

"Badly in need of a weekend down on the farm," Salinger replied, speaking into the headset microphone. A restricted circuit gave the two an element of privacy.

"Some farm, this Haworth Manor of yours," Dominique said.

"Yeah," Salinger admitted, recalling the walled fortress his family called home.

As the two fell into a round of small talk, Jack Salinger felt bitter. He knew that his feelings for his attractive pilot were unacceptable and extremely dangerous, but he also knew they were genuine. In a world of sex machines and stimulants, Salinger was aware that he was very much in love with Dominique Cantrell. His feelings were all the more inexplicable considering the very limited contact he'd had with Dominique. Salinger had interviewed Major Cantrell when she had been assigned to his security force. That interview had been the only time Dominique had not been dressed in a flight suit, but his response to her could only be what was once called "love at first sight."

Why should feelings of such intensity and tenderness be illegal and prohibited?

Jack Salinger asked himself this question every time he had contact with her.

Salinger's father was one of the most vocal advocates of restrictions on intimate interactions between the economic subclasses of Angels. Salinger recalled many heated arguments he'd had with his father about this issue. As usual, the professor had overwhelmed him with a barrage of sophisticated chicanery.

Not once in his life had he ever let Jack beat him at anything.

As the chopper passed through earthling airspace, Salinger tried to concentrate on the scene passing below the aircraft. Expansive Angel estates swept past his eyes. He could make out the forms of earthlings working the fields surrounding the walled manor houses. An occasional village broke the monotony of the passing scene. The spires of churches floated past the chopper. A few transport vehicles sped along the major roads, carrying earthlings to and from the collective farms and the factories located near the larger cities, where those not assigned to the smaller estates and villages were employed. Appropriately, the Angels of America traveled by air; earthlings rarely left the ground.

"Any interesting patients since I saw you last?" Dominique asked.

"As a matter of fact," Salinger responded, "the President of the United States consulted me recently."

"Oh my," Dominique said, "I know her job must be stressful, but I would think she would have her own private psychotherapist. What could our Madam President possibly want with you, Dr. Salinger?"

Salinger had shared some of his more eccentric patients with Dominique during previous flights. She was happy to play along with him in reference to this latest rather imaginative case.

"She was a party girl, looking for a supply of happy pills."

Dominique laughed. "Be sure to let me know if she pesters you again."

Suddenly, a cockpit alarm sounded. Major Cantrell barked into the headsets of all three of her passengers.

"Hold on, people, we have an incoming!"

Salinger could see the contrail of the surface-to-air missile snaking toward them. His body was jerked to the side, as Dominique activated the chopper's defensive shields and took immediate evasive action. The missile shot past harmlessly, a hundred yards off the starboard side of the chopper, and then exploded amid a cluster of thermal flares Major Cantrell had launched.

Cantrell punched in a few numbers using the onboard computer keyboard. The chopper went into a steep dive, retracing the path of the SAM. At the appropriate moment, Dominique fired.

Jack Salinger watched the twin projectiles leave the nose of the chopper, pick up speed as they locked onto the target, and then race toward the earth. He watched the cockpit screen as the two detonations vaporized the launch site and surrounding terrain. The missile had been fired from a remote area, at some distance from any habitations. A dark cloud of smoke and debris swept past the chopper's windshield.

"Where the hell are they getting these damn things?" the security patrol's commanding officer spat into his headset microphone with frustration. "This is the fourth strike I've been involved in this quarter. These old SAMs may be antiquated, but with luck the bastards are going to take one of us down some day."

"The stats show a steady increase in hostile activity," Major Cantrell admitted.

"We'll get them," the commander assured the group. "And when we do, the executions will be spectacular. You can bet your asses on that!"

Major Cantrell radioed the appropriate coordinates to her command post. Retaliatory saturation bombing of the earthling settlement closest to the launch site would take place in minutes.

CHAPTER 10

▼

Following the attempted missile strike, the rest of the flight into Haworth Manor should have been uneventful.

"You know, you really look sexy today," Dominique crooned into her microphone. "I can't seem to take my eyes off of you."

Salinger yearned to reciprocate.

Dominique reached over and placed her hand on Salinger's knee. Major Cantrell had never done anything like this before.

Salinger, with some embarrassment, gently removed Dominique's hand. His skin remained warm and tingly where her hand had rested, however. Cantrell's gesture was unnerving. He was relieved when the familiar façade of the family compound came into view.

From the air, the turreted walls of Haworth Manor looked reassuring and unassailable. The Edwardian Style mansion rose skyward from a central courtyard with elegant grace. Major Cantrell obtained clearance for landing from the security forces on the ground. The chopper then descended across a meandering moat and over the massive stone wall to the heliport where the aircraft gently set down.

Salinger tried to give Dominique the usual gratuity, but she refused to accept his present. Instead she pressed a small object into his hand, as he was disembarking from the chopper. Salinger glanced at what she had given him. He was shocked to find an identification card containing Dominique's personal access numbers, including the code to the private telecommunication module in her living space.

Salinger stood dumbfounded as he watched the chopper lift off. He waved meekly in reply to the hand blown kiss Dominique Cantrell directed toward him as the aircraft banked and then sped off into the distance.

Jack Salinger walked slowly across the courtyard toward the entryway to the mansion, where his mother stood waiting for him. Two large ravens eyed him with suspicion. He was troubled by Major Cantrell's recklessness. She knew the penalties for interclass liaisons as well as he did. And yet, she had clearly initiated inappropriate physical contact and had even hinted at intimacy. Salinger knew he should either destroy the card, or forward the evidence to the central authorities at the Department of Homeland Security. In the days ahead, however, Jack Salinger would do neither.

Salinger passed several of the estate's hirelings as he approached the main house. As was expected, these privileged earthlings directed their eyes to the ground, avoiding any direct eye contact with a superior. Salinger glanced up at the massive barrier that separated his family home from the outside world. One of the Angel guards saluted, as Salinger passed below his post. Although he was not expected to return the greeting, Dr. Salinger graced the sentry with a friendly wave.

Salinger bounded up the curved flight of stairs leading to the massive portico of the house. His mother, Nora, was standing in the foyer and fidgeted impatiently as her youngest son's retinas were scanned. Then she greeted him warmly.

"Jack, darling, it's so good to have you home. Happy birthday!"

"It's good to be here, Mother," he admitted. "I've missed you."

"Your father is a prig to insist that you work in that infernal city," Nora pouted. "I can't see why you can't move back here. You could run your silly practice from home, you know."

"We've been through all of that before," Salinger said. "Besides, I think Father is right. I need to establish my independence."

The fact that Jack Salinger's father *was* right about most things was irritating, but he suppressed the emotion in deference to his mother.

"Pooh," Nora Salinger said, as she escorted Jack into the main lobby of the house. "You should move back home."

"Who's on the guest list for the weekend?" Salinger asked, as his mother led him to the drawing room.

"Well, Marla, naturally. And an English diplomat your father will be tutoring. You may have heard of him, Jack. His name is Alfred Dobson, the son of Field Marshall Sir Charles Dobson. Young Alfred is a bit of a snob, but he asks the most outrageous questions. I'm sure he exasperates your father beyond measure. Charlotte is here, but Martin is off on business and can't get back until early tomorrow morning. Our big party for you will be Saturday evening."

Marla LaBaron was Jack Salinger's betrothed. George Salinger had selected his youngest son's mate from one of the finest Seraphim families. Salinger had winced when his mother had mentioned Marla's name. He realized his animosity toward Marla personally was not justified. She was a stunningly attractive woman who was witty and intelligent. He was a far luckier man than many of his contemporaries. A LaBaron bonding, and the substantial dowry Marla would bring to the match, would add greatly to the family's fortune. Jack would be able to repay his debt to the Salinger estate. Marla was also healthy and could be expected to bring heirs, should Martin and Charlotte fail to do so.

Jack's parents were concerned about Martin's situation, in fact. In three years, Jack's elder brother and his life mate had not been able to produce an heir. Charlotte's first two pregnancies had resulted in one early abortion and a stillborn male. Extensive testing at University Lying-in Hospital for Angels indicated the problem was Charlotte's. She was capable of impregnation, but she had been unable to carry her pregnancies to term. Martin's sperm counts were reported to be normal. Salinger had tried to hack into his brother's personal files during an earlier visit to Haworth Manor, but he had not been successful.

Should Charlotte become pregnant again, she would be confined to bed during her third attempt at bringing the gestation to term. Charlotte realized this could be her final chance. She had become irritable and extremely emotional since the failure of her second pregnancy. Jack had tried to cheer Charlotte up, kidding that she should log on to his web site for treatment. The highly anticipated third pregnancy had not yet occurred.

Marla LaBaron was much more robust than Charlotte Salinger. During the Middle Ages, she would have been judged an excellent breeder, even before the fact. As Jack Salinger thought of Marla LaBaron, however, he could not drive images of Dominique Cantrell's face and body from his mind.

Nora Salinger swept into the drawing room on the arm of her youngest son. The greetings and introductions were dramatic, as was usual when Nora was in her element.

George Salinger was sipping a glass of champagne as Jack was ushered into the drawing room. He placed his drink on a coaster and folded both arms across his chest. He did not greet Salinger with any enthusiasm.

"Did you bring the spread sheet data for the practice?" he asked.

"Yes, Sir," Salinger responded. "As you insisted, Father."

Salinger immediately felt chagrined at his deferential demeanor when addressing the professor. He would have preferred to throw the disc containing the financial data into his father's face.

Jack's mother stood at her husband's side, smiling at Salinger with obvious affection and pride.

Salinger had never been able to understand what his mother saw in her husband. Nora's affection for George Salinger stuck in Jack's throat. He was forced to admit, but only with reluctance, that the professor was a man capable of inspiring love in other human beings.

Marla greeted Jack affectionately. She pressed the palm of his hand with familiarity and kissed him gently on the cheek. He tried to feel some emotional response to her, but he was unable. Fortunately, he and Marla were not yet expected to be intimate. He was certain he would have difficulty responding to her sexually, although he suspected Marla was hoping he might visit her room clandestinely this weekend, so she could perhaps give him a special birthday gift. They were to be bonded in the fall, in the month of September.

Salinger felt uncomfortable through the cocktail hour. The conversation was basically a description for Alfred Dobson's benefit of Haworth Manor, its security systems, and the functions of the various earthlings employed at the "farm," as Professor Salinger repeatedly called the home and sprawling grounds. Jack noticed that his father withheld a description of the concealed passageway into and out of the manor that was known to family members alone.

Salinger could not drive the brief and reckless physical contact Dominique Cantrell had initiated from his mind. Curiously, his skin still tingled where she had touched him earlier. He was beginning to regret that he had come home when dinner was finally announced, relieving him of his uneasiness momentarily.

Jack toyed with his food, as the seemingly endless seven-course meal wore on.

Marla, Charlotte, and Nora were invited to join the after dinner conversation, but the three women retired to the sitting room, Nora Salinger expressing displeasure with the "horrid political discussions" the men in her life enjoyed.

Alfred Dobson had been standing comfortably with his forearm resting on the ornate Victorian mantle of the fireplace. He returned to the table and took his seat. He was one of only a few men able to look down on George Salinger. Jack noticed, however, that when agitated Dobson would rake his close cropped blonde hair with his fingers. He was impeccably dressed in a Royal Air Force uniform. Several tiers of brightly colored decorations, pinned to Dobson's breast, attested to his prowess in the skies over England. Although he and Jack were the same age, Dobson was a great deal more self-assured.

Alfred Dobson went on the offensive as soon as the women had left the room.

"You were trying to justify your government's policies in the Middle East earlier this afternoon, Professor Salinger, but I'm afraid you have not convinced me that the strategy the United States employed during that conflict would meet any test of human morality."

Jack sat watching his father tamp tobacco into a well-tempered meerschaum. He recalled his recent patient—Reeves may have been the name—with the hookah. But of course the professor would never...

"Human morality has always been relative, Alfred," George Salinger said. "The history of your own nation should leave you little doubt of that."

"I will admit British colonial policies, even in America, were often ill-advised," Dobson conceded, "but our crimes, shall we say, pale in comparison with yours."

"We fought the war against terrorism the only way we could," Jack suggested.

"Ah, but were you fighting against terrorism or for oil?" Alfred asked. "That has always been the nagging question in regard to America's foreign policy in the Middle East."

"We fought that war for both reasons, as you clearly know," Jack said. He glanced briefly at his father, who was passively monitoring the exchange as he lit his bowl.

"Any discussion of morality is actually moot, Alfred," Professor Salinger interjected, parrying toward the Englishman with the stem of his pipe. "You've read Thucydides. I ask you to recall his beautiful description of the Melian conference during the Peloponnesian War. The Athenians made no justification for their treatment of the Melians, because they simply did not have to. The Athenians were the superior force, they made their demands, and they responded appropriately to Melian resistance. We were the superior force in the Middle East; we did what we had to do, and we need make no excuses for our actions at all."

George Salinger sent a cloud of smoke wafting in Dobson's direction.

"The end—from one's own relative point of view, of course—always justifies the means. Is that what you are implying?"

Dobson's face had reddened noticeably.

"Exactly," Jack said. "We are no longer threatened by acts of terror from an ideology that no longer exists as a political force and we have an unlimited supply of oil."

Jack rose from his chair and ambled toward an ornate coffee urn sitting on a side table.

"And before you get self-righteous, Alfred," he said over his shoulder as he refreshed his cup, "remember my father's suggestion that you consider the history of your own country. Think what England did to the Irish, as the most egregious example of many."

Salinger could not help looking to his father for approval. The professor's face displayed a vacuous smile. As was typical, he could not bring himself to offer his youngest son the smallest sop.

"We didn't use nuclear weapons on seventeen cities!" Dobson said heatedly. "We didn't put all of the males who survived our invasion of Ireland to death, and we didn't enslave all of the remaining women and children!"

"But my dear, Alfred," Professor Salinger said, emphasizing his point with several thrusts of the meerschaum. "With the exception of the use of nuclear weapons, that is exactly how the Athenians dealt with the Melians, and the actions of our Grecian predecessors were appropriate to the situation. We were similarly justified in dealing with the egregious terrorist attacks against us that emanated from the Middle East."

As Jack regained his seat, he fixed on the wry smile that had passed over his father's face.

"The weapons available to the Greeks were simply more primitive than those available to us," the professor added. "We Americans, you see, have finally begun to learn something from history."

Dobson spat, his normally placid features contorted with rage.

"Well, there is no precedent in our treatment of the Irish that can possibly compare with the genocide of an entire people and the outright rape of the largest oil bearing region on the planet!"

Jack Salinger slammed his fist onto the table.

"No, Alfred, England confined its rape and pillage to the Catholic population of Ireland," he said. "Keep in mind, the United States did not initiate nuclear warfare. We were attacked first. Don't sit there and tell me that your country would not have used nuclear weapons in the Middle East had you been in our position," he added sarcastically. "With the exception of the destruction of Westminster Abbey, you British were relatively spared the outrageous losses the terrorists inflicted on us."

Jack looked at his father. The professor puffed placidly, revealing nothing Jack could interpret as approval.

"You know, Alfred, you're just miffed that England is now one of our client states, instead of a world power," Salinger continued. "And yet, you buy our oil and you trade technology and surplus goods with us without compunction. It would seem monetary issues always supplant moral ones in the end. Great Britain is no better in that regard than the rest of the European Commonwealth of Nations."

Dobson wiped at his mouth and then threw his napkin onto the dining table.

"Without my country's help during the early stages of your war against terrorism, the United States would not be in the position it's in now," Alfred countered. "Think how close you came to losing everything when China threatened to intervene," he added.

"Admittedly, the outcome of the war might have been drastically different had the Chinese interceded," Professor Salinger said, with reflection. "But, like the Russians before them during John F. Kennedy's famous 13 days, the Chinese blinked. We have acquiesced in their usurpation of hegemony in Asia and they have wisely chosen not to interfere with our foreign policy in Europe and the Middle East.

"But remember, Alfred, we appreciate your nation's assistance beyond measure," Professor Salinger added, his expression friendly and engaging, the pipe now a calumet. "Look at the gesture of respect for English politics we took at the time of our domestic coup by retaining the symbolic office of president, a figurehead with duties modeled exactly on those of your own archaic king.

"We're also especially grateful for the role your magnificent father played during the years of our great struggle, Alfred. England is our mother nation and will always have a warm place in the American heart, as will any member of the Dobson family."

The two younger men accepted Professor Salinger's remark as an invitation to a momentary truce while they puffed on cigars and sipped a glass of Cockburn's Special Reserve port. But Alfred Dobson was not ready to end the exchange.

"Let me ask you this, Jack," he said, as his cigar tip flamed before his face. "You say you are no longer in danger of acts of terrorism from alternative ideologies, as you expressed it. How then, do you explain the attempted missile strike that you described so eloquently, and so heatedly, earlier this evening?"

"You know, Dobson, I sometimes wonder how you managed a security clearance to visit this country," Salinger challenged.

"Make no mistake," Alfred said, "I love the United States of America as much as you do. I'm just concerned about your future. And since the prospects for my own country are so closely tied to yours, that means I'm worried about England's future too. Every nation in history, no matter how strong, has managed to self-destruct eventually. What makes you think your plutocracy is immune?"

Dobson followed the remark by lifting his glass in a mock toast.

"Because we've swept away all petty moral concerns and will always do exactly what we have to do to ensure that no force—whether external or internal—will ever destroy us," said Professor Salinger, interrupting Jack's attempted response.

"That sounds like a remark the Athenian delegation might have made to the Melians, Professor, and you well know there is no Athenian Empire today," Dobson suggested.

"True," George Salinger admitted, emptying the bowl of his pipe into an ashtray. "Your point is well taken. But America today is not the Athens of the 5th century BCE, Alfred. The Athenians controlled a paltry region extending from Attica to Ionia. We control the most strategic oil bearing region in the world. And within our own borders, we have eliminated any threat of meaningful revolt. Crackpots will always insist on making feeble efforts at intimidating us, but with no practical consequences."

"We have never lost a single aircraft to the antiquated missiles the earthlings have managed to fire at us," Salinger assured Alfred.

"There is always a first time," Dobson insisted. "Think of the propaganda value the enslaved millions of Americans would derive from even a single success."

George Salinger placed both hands on the table and leaned toward his guest.

"The enlightenment I'm going to provide you during your sabbatical with me, Alfred, will address the methods we have evolved to control our less valued citizens. Your mentors at home have charged me with an important task. The time is not far off when absolute separation of the economic elite from the rest of the population will have to occur in your own country, as happened here in the United States.

"You are held in great esteem, Alfred. Because of your own merits, I might add, and not just because of your illustrious father."

Salinger winced at the poorly disguised significance of his father's remark.

"I'm told that many influential people in England feel that you have the unique talents necessary to accomplish the economic reorganization of British society," the professor continued. "Some have serious doubts about your resolve, however. The hope is that under my tutelage you may be purged of some of the more primitive ideas you have expressed tonight."

"For your sake, Dobson, and the sake of your family, I hope you get with the program," Salinger said.

Dobson's eyes narrowed ominously.

"Are you threatening me?" he demanded.

"Me? Why no, Dobson," Jack said. "I'm not threatening you. Personally, I don't give a damn what happens to you."

Professor Salinger directed a condescending smile toward his son.

"You must be more gracious to our guest, Jack," he said.

CHAPTER 11

▼

Following the heated after-dinner conversation with Alfred Dobson, Jack Salinger felt more jaded than before. Typically, he had failed to impress his father.

The party watched the state sponsored national newscast and then the *Friday Night Fights*. One of the combatants scored her 12th consecutive victory and won retirement to the islands.

"I'm so happy for that young woman's mother," Nora Salinger said.

George Salinger was the only person in the room who knew the truth about the islands of blissful retirement. Earthlings who managed to survive the televised trials by combat were exiled to places that made the conditions on the ancient French prison at Devil's Island pale in comparison. Because of the scarcity of food supplies, earthlings in the penal colonies were often forced to engage in cannibalism.

The inmates were segregated by gender and according to sexual preference. The populations of the various islands were seeded from time to time with males or females—as the case might require—afflicted with leprosy or the advanced stages of the various sexually transmitted diseases. When necessary, population control was effected by introducing some more virulent infection harvested from one of the mainland's inner cities.

Of those viewing the post fight festivities that evening, only Professor Salinger could have imagined the shocked disbelief of a victorious earthling arriving at one of the penal colonies. Such life sentences represented the Council of Twelve's final irony applied to earthlings daring to commit crimes against Angels.

As the family watched the victory celebration, the jubilant young woman was escorted from the arena amid a flurry of fireworks and confetti.

"You know, Dobson," George Salinger said, "there has not been a televised execution of an Angel for treason in over eight years. Wouldn't you agree that validates our new American order?"

Dobson appeared to be inordinately interested in his drink. He said nothing.

Salinger begged off participating in the rest of the evening's activities, claiming indisposition. Marla was terribly disappointed that Jack would not hear her piano recital. She had planned to play Pachelbel's *Canon in D* especially for him.

In his room, Salinger lit up another Mary J and poured himself a snifter of Remy Martin Centaur XO. He regretted certain consequences of his engagement. He recalled a simpler time when visits home had been more enjoyable. Before his betrothal to Marla, he would have spent the night with Loreena.

Salinger remembered the night his mother had sent Loreena to him, a special gift on his sixteenth birthday. Jack had been terrified when the nubile fourteen-year-old unexpectedly appeared in his room, bearing a palm top with a note of greeting from his mother.

"I hope you will enjoy my little gift. Love, Mother."

Loreena naturally refused to make eye contact with Salinger initially. She kept her eyes averted to the floor, as all earthlings were required to do when addressing Angels.

But then Loreena opened her gown. Salinger had used a few of the machines, but the sight of young woman's supple nakedness had terrified him. He ordered her to leave his room.

"Please, young Jack, don't reject me," she cried, throwing herself at his knees. "If I fail to please you, they'll send me beyond the walls. I'd die there."

Many pleasurable nights with Loreena had followed.

Loreena had been sold as an infant to Haworth Manor by her parents, in exchange for a monthly allotment of food and imported beer. Free intercourse between earthlings and Angels was prohibited for reasons of social stability, but also because sexually transmitted diseases were rampant in the non-segregated earthling communities. Loreena had been sterilized prior to puberty to prevent interclass fertilization. She had also been carefully isolated from any human sexual contact until her assignment to Salinger.

Her life in the Salinger compound had been one of relative ease. She had been well educated. Her virginity had been sacrificed to one of the machines. In order to service a young Angel male properly—which was the purpose of her adoption by the Salinger family—Loreena needed a high level of sexual sophistication. She progressed to expert level on the most advanced machines available.

Once Jack Salinger had accepted her, Loreena became responsible for his own sexual education, making certain he would always be an effective lover, able to pleasure any woman completely. In appreciation, Jack Salinger had graciously allowed full eye contact during his liaisons with his earthling friend.

Because the idea was alien to him and simply out of the question, Jack Salinger had never fallen in love with Loreena.

He recalled his last meeting with the young woman.

"I'm engaged to be bonded," he brusquely informed her. "We can never be together again."

Loreena said nothing. She looked into his eyes. As he returned her gaze, the pain she could not hide suggested that Loreena had not been immune to falling in love with him.

The cognac and the marijuana alleviated Salinger's despondency considerably. He toyed with the idea of making a foray to Marla's room. He knew she would be overjoyed, but his recollection of being with Loreena had conjured fantasies of bedding Dominique Cantrell, not Marla LaBaron. Salinger was thinking about pulling one of his old machines out of the closet, but opted for self-imposed celibacy instead. He felt chivalrous pride in this courtly sacrifice for Dominique.

Salinger needed rest. Jack's father had organized a morning hunt. Personally, Jack hated hunting and was able to avoid using a weapon because of his profession. Jack was the "conscientious objector" of the family. His father took great pride in his own prowess at hunting, however, and insisted that both of his sons ride with him into the field.

Suddenly, Salinger was aware of a prickling sensation at the back of his neck. In fact, he dreaded the coming hunt. He wiped a few beads of sweat from his forehead and lay quietly, monitoring his rising heartbeat with clinical detachment.

He recalled his first hunt, as a boy of ten.

"For the love of Plutus, fire Jack!" his father demanded.

The front sight of the rifle was jerking before his eyes, but Jack could see nothing beyond the barrel of the gun. He could not focus on the rapidly moving target, but he managed to pull the trigger. The weapon jammed into his shoulder painfully and knocked him to the ground. Martin brought down Jack's quarry with an ear splitting blast.

"Pick yourself up, you worthless whelp," his father yelled. "You make me sick, Jack. You're no Salinger! You're all O'Connor and the runt of the litter to boot. If I didn't love your mother so much, I'd despise her for bringing you into existence. Martin, teach this worm a lesson in manliness."

Martin, his face radiating perverse joy, jerked Jack to his feet and then knocked him back down.

"Get up," Martin shouted.

Jack cowered beneath Martin's onslaught. He groveled before his much larger brother.

"I'll clean your rifle, Martin," he whimpered. "Please, don't hit me so hard."

"Sure," Martin said. "Get up."

Jack staggered to his feet. A crushing blow struck the side of his head felling him again.

Salinger ground his thumbnail into his palm until he drew blood. He tried to concentrate on images of stomping horses, and the sounds of baying hounds. Slowly, his agitation subsided. He was finally able to sleep.

CHAPTER 12

▼

Marla LaBaron waited until past midnight, but Jack Salinger did not come to her room. She realized Jack did not love her, but she could not understand why. She had been told clearly during her pre-engagement interview with Nora Salinger that Jack was not a homosexual. She found him extremely attractive, but nothing Marla did seemed to arouse her prospective mate sexually.

Marla undressed and stood before the full-length mirror in her room. She loved to look at her body, especially in soft lighting like this. She caressed her breasts and then reached down and began to massage her clitoris gently, very gently. Marla was convinced that Jack Salinger was a complete fool.

Marla LaBaron felt fortunate to be living in contemporary America. Marla was a free woman thanks in part to her prospective father-in-law, whom she adored without reservation. She had no restrictions whatsoever regarding her choice of a career. No field of study or vocation was closed to her. But Marla LaBaron had chosen to become a mother. She wanted fine children to nurture and love.

Motherhood, for Marla, was sacred. She had searched the fairs of the antique sellers for old rosaries and had learned to chant the old litany. No one knew of her secret devotions to the cult of Mary.

She realized that in another era, her life might have been miserable, even unbearable. She might have had a similarly arranged bonding with a philandering unloving life mate who could have infected her with some dreadful disease. In another age, she may have suffered sexual frustration and she may have aged prematurely from lack of attention.

Modern America was a compelling place for female Angels, thanks to men like George Salinger. Marla had no fear of sexually transmitted disease, unwanted pregnancy, or—most importantly—sexual neglect. Second Independence Day was Marla's La Baron's favorite holiday. She gave thanks almost every day of her life to Plutus, and to Professor Salinger, for the modern world order.

Marla was fully aroused now. She was ready. She was also very angry with Jack Salinger. Once the engagement had been announced, Marla's parents had ordered her to forego any further pre-bonding intercourse with the segregated male earthlings available to her, but she was permitted unlimited use of the machines. Machine sex was not considered adultery. She carefully attached the sensors, then the electrodes, and mounted the appliance. Her fingers trembling with excitement, Marla managed to activate the miraculous machine.

An hour later, sweaty and spent, Marla too fell to restful untroubled sleep. She dreamed of cherubic children dancing in fields teeming with wild flowers.

CHAPTER 13

▼

Jack's father summoned him to the library shortly after breakfast. Marla LaBaron and Alfred Dobson had opted to sleep late. Jack's brother, Martin, was sipping Grace Rare tea as Jack entered the ornate room. Volumes bound in fine Moroccan leather filled floor-to-ceiling bookshelves.

"Come in," Professor Salinger said, glancing up as Jack entered the room. "I've been going over your accounts with Martin and we agree, the practice is going well."

"I'm glad you're pleased, Sir," Salinger said. "How are you, Martin?"

"Welcome home, little brother," Martin said. He had that familiar disdainful expression on his face that Salinger would have loved to rip off and shove down his brother's throat.

Salinger busied himself at the coffee urn. He could feel the eyes of the two older men boring into him, always assessing, always disappointed.

"What do you think of Dobson?" his father asked.

"I don't like his attitude," Salinger admitted, turning to confront the professor. "He seems quite liberal, don't you think?"

"Come now, Jack, I seem to recall someone else who once wanted to bring justice and fairness to all people on the planet," Martin chided. "How easily you forget your stint as a rebel Angel. Remember me, the son who remained dutifully at home and who authorized the funds that were needed to keep you from losing your head?"

"You don't have to rub your generosity into my face, Martin," Jack snapped.

"Come now, Jack, let's have none of that," the Professor admonished.

Salinger forced himself to cool off. He would gain nothing by antagonizing Martin. He *did* owe a great deal to his older brother.

"Dobson has a lean and hungry look," Jack said. "You recall what was said of Cassius. He thinks too much. Such men are dangerous. What the hell is Dobson really doing here?"

"Alfred Dobson is in a position to lead England into the final stages of the development of that country's own plutocracy," George Salinger replied. "He has capitalized beautifully on his late father's reputation. But, as I intimated last evening, some influential compatriots of Dobson's have serious doubts about his commitment. Those who support Dobson feel he needs to get some hands-on experience of the advantages of a two-tiered society, for those of us at the top, at any rate.

"As a matter of fact, your mother sent Dobson that earthling last night, the one you used to bed now and then. Loreena, I think her name is?"

Salinger winced.

"From the look on your face, Jack," Martin laughed, "You must still be infatuated with the pretty wench. I tried to get a couple of nights with her myself, but Mother wouldn't hear of it. She said the maiden was yours exclusively."

Since his engagement to Marla LaBaron, Salinger had no right to be concerned about Loreena. Still, he was galled to think of Alfred Dobson having sex with his former bedmate.

"Well, let's hope he doesn't infect her," Jack said. "I don't trust the English health care system."

"What if he does?" Professor Salinger said, with a laugh. "Your mother tells me the woman is getting on in years a little—nearly twenty-eight, I think Nora said. She will have to be let go eventually."

Loreena had entered the pool of body servants assigned to guests since Jack's engagement. She would be monitored carefully for sexually transmitted infection after every contact. Infection, or an unfavorable performance report, were—in either case—grounds for her immediate dismissal from Haworth Manor.

"I hope a night of rutting between the sheets will have calmed Dobson down. I noticed he didn't make it down for breakfast," Professor Salinger said with a smile. "How was she, by the way?"

Salinger peered into his coffee cup, concentrating on the dregs.

"She was fair," he lied.

Jack tried to bend his spoon, but the object resisted.

Who ran away with a spoon?

"So what do you really know about Dobson?" Jack asked, looking into his father's less than friendly face.

"I'm sure we don't know enough," Professor Salinger replied. "Let us just say he will bear careful watching."

"He's a puzzle," Martin said. "I've spoken to Kurt Striker, our Director of Homeland Security. Intelligence on Dobson is giving mixed signals. He's either an innocent English patriot who is putting on a show, or a quite sinister force to be reckoned with. I agree with Father. Striker will continue to monitor Dobson closely and will keep us posted."

Martin quaffed his tea.

"I've got to check on the falcons," he said, rising from his chair.

Jack emptied his own cup and was also about to leave, but his father checked him.

"I want to speak to you," he said. "Privately."

"What is it?" Salinger asked, after Martin had left the room. He was always uncomfortable when interrogated by George Salinger.

"What's going on between you and Miranda Lee-Weston?"

The sudden reference to the president took Salinger aback. His hesitation was the cue George Salinger was waiting for.

"I demand that you tell me everything. Every detail."

Salinger picked up his coffee cup, hoping to find some residual liquid there.

"There's nothing to tell, Sir," he said, slowly replacing the cup on the table.

"Don't lie to me!" his father thundered.

"I really have no idea what you're talking about, Father."

"You were contacted by Mrs. Lee-Weston. Shortly thereafter, you visited your local Museum of Computer History. I want to know why."

"You know, I do recall some crackpot drug seeker who tried to pawn herself off as the President of the United States," Jack said, choosing each word deliberately. He was beginning to enjoy himself. "I assure you, Father, I didn't take her seriously. Why don't you sweep my hard drive? You won't find any contacts there from Madam Lee-Weston."

The rage playing over George Salinger's face had blossomed into crimson blotches.

Don't lose control, Father. Plutus forbid, you might have a stroke.

"I don't think you understand the seriousness of this affair, Jack," the Professor said. "I will never allow you to compromise this family again. If necessary, I will kill you with my bare hands."

"Your love for me is boundless, isn't it Father?"

George Salinger rose from his seat and moved to the rear of Jack's chair, gripping the wings of the upright. Salinger could see the whitened knuckles of his father's hands at either side of his face.

"Miranda Lee-Weston is not in the same league with Kurt Striker," the professor said. He was speaking with deliberation, trying to maintain control. "Striker will eat her alive, when the time comes. You would be wise, Jack, to put a bullet in your brain rather than continue playing this little diversion with our foolhardy Madam President."

"Were I to do that, Father—put a bullet in my brain—would I finally make you happy?"

George Salinger said nothing. He slowly eased his grip and then stormed out of the room.

CHAPTER 14

▼

The hunt later that morning began gloriously. The weather was fine and the animals were in superb form. The local health status remained code green. The riders were permitted light clothing and the tactile pleasure of a galloping horse beneath one's legs. The group trotted through the gateway in the outer wall, over the bridge that arched above the moat surrounding the manor, and out into the countryside. Dobson looked a little tired, but he was in better spirits and did not raise any contentious issues during the short ride over to the staging area.

As he cantered along beside Martin and behind Dobson and the professor, Salinger surveyed the occupants of the four security vehicles that were accompanying the hunting party. He was still morose. The prospect of the coming hunt did little to lift his spirits.

All of the security guards were Angels. Most of them had been with the family for years and appeared to be completely loyal. But the sixteen men accompanying the party that morning were extremely well armed. They carried far more firepower than the hunters did.

Salinger thought about what Dobson had said the previous evening, in light of his recent interaction with Miranda Lee-Weston. Most Angels were convinced earthlings were incapable of mounting any sustained resistance. Until recently, Salinger would have agreed. The SAM attacks, for instance, were likely to remain ineffective. Like most enslaved people, the earthlings had to release their rage periodically. Breaking into outdated weapons depots and then setting off a few ineffective fireworks probably brought some solace to the oppressed.

But what if Mrs. Lee-Weston was able to recruit serious opposition to the plutocracy? What if the president managed to gain support from some outside force?

What if significant numbers of Angels joined a resistance movement initiated by earthlings under the president's command? A well-coordinated action might catalyze a regional or even a nationwide revolt.

Salinger tried to make eye contact with as many of the guards as possible, as the security vehicles rode along beside his prancing stallion. He was not able to read anything in the stony faces he probed. Each man seemed grimly determined to do his duty.

A herd of white tailed deer grazing near a line of trees bounded into the woods as the convoy approached the staging area. The vehicles came to a halt. The chief of the regional earthling police force stood waiting before several primitive wooden cages mounted atop carts. The hunting party dismounted and then made ready their weapons. Martin retrieved a falcon, directing the talons of the hooded bird to the leather sheath that covered his left forearm.

George Salinger paid the police chief two cases of high quality imported Danish beer, far superior to the government issued lager most of the earthlings drank. The disbursement was very generous, considering the value of the occupants of the cages.

"What brings our subjects to such a pass?" the professor asked.

"A rough bunch, this group" the chief said. As he spoke, the man carefully avoided the professor's eyes. "They've been carrying on a regular reign of terror. Had you not sent for them, my lord, we would have hung them ourselves."

"Thievery alone, or murder and mayhem?" Martin Salinger asked.

"Every crime in the book," the chief responded.

Alfred Dobson had moved to the cages and was peering at the incarcerated criminals.

"Well," George Salinger said, "let's get on with it."

The occupants of the first cage were released. They stood watching the group of hunters. One of the pair, a young woman, was shaking uncontrollably.

"Well, me lovelies," the chief said. "You have been found guilty and are about to be sentenced. Do you have any last words?"

The male earthling spat in the chief's direction.

"I didn't think so," the chief said. He pointed out a line of trees some 100 yards distant. "Now, by the rules of engagement you have a chance to save yourselves. You'll be given a generous head start. If you can reach the forest, you may be able to survive this little exercise in American justice. So, off with you now."

The two prisoners bolted in the direction of the thicket. After a short delay, Martin Salinger and his father released the falcons.

Falconry was one of Martin Salinger's favorite sports. He had studied the treatise on the subject written in the 13th century by Fredrick II.

The birds flew in pursuit of the two runners and each falcon quickly bound to its victim, bringing the pair tumbling to the ground amid a swirl of thrashing hands and wings. The peregrines at Haworth Manor had been specially trained to go for the eyes. The screams of the young couple were strident as the birds did their merciless work.

The falcons were recalled. The two prisoners were staggering about the open field several hundred feet away.

"Which one do you want, Dobson?" Martin asked. "Oedipus or Jocasta?"

Dobson's jaw muscles clenched. He gripped his weapon tightly. For an instant, Salinger thought he saw the barrel of Dobson's rifle move in Martin's direction. But then Dobson turned and walked slowly back toward the awaiting trucks.

"I'll take the girl," Professor Salinger said.

Father and son took aim at their respective targets and fired almost simultaneously. Martin seemed intent on making an unassailable statement to counter Alfred Dobson's spinelessness. He took ruthless aim at his quarry.

Martin's shot took off the right side of the young man's head. His victim dropped face first to the ground like a felled tree. Professor Salinger's shot caught the young woman smartly beneath the left breast. She stood bolt upright momentarily, as if surprised she had been shot. She uttered no sound. Her hands clutched at her chest briefly before she too fell heavily to the earth. The girl's partner continued to convulse on the ground for several moments.

With each subsequent pair of prisoners, the elder Salingers held the falcons somewhat longer, giving the accused a larger lead, increasing the sport of the hunt. A variation from a freestanding shooting position was pursuit of the runners on horseback and shooting the pursued from the saddle. Jack could see his father's reflexes were slowing. One of the prisoners, badly wounded but alive, made the line of trees and had to be hunted down by the dogs. Martin Salinger brought the treed female to the ground with a savage gut shot that tore out the liver and a large segment of intestine.

Salinger's father badgered him relentlessly to participate, but Jack sarcastically cited his profession as an excuse to beg off. Alfred Dobson also refused to take part in the hunt that morning. Professor Salinger was equally appalled by the reluctance of the Englishman.

"I wonder what Field Marshall Dobson would think of your conduct, Alfred?" the Professor chided.

Dobson glared at George Salinger, but maintained icy silence.

Salinger sensed rivulets of sweat running down the insides of his arms. The sun was quickly moving toward the meridian. He ticked off the minutes as the relentless hunt wore on. Finally, the carnage was over.

"Send the dogs back to the farm when they've finished," Professor Salinger said. "They haven't been fed since Wednesday, so I suspect they'll be at them a while yet."

"Aye, aye," the chief responded with a smart salute.

When the trucks had been loaded, the party began the ride back to the main house. Martin's returning falcon glided smoothly to a landing on his forearm as the riders trotted toward home. Jack looked back at the staging area. His father's bird was perched on the forehead of one of the victims, the peregrine still at work on the nearly empty eye sockets of the woman's bleeding face.

CHAPTER 15

▼

Jack's mother welcomed the returning party of hunters and led the group to a delectable lunch in the garden pavilion featuring marinated octopus, stone crab claws, and Scottish smoked salmon.

"How many did you bag, Darling?" Nora Salinger asked her husband.

"Twelve I think, all together. But Martin had to come to my assistance and finish off one of mine," the professor responded. "I guess I'm getting old."

Jack was hungry and washed down his lunch with several chilled glasses of a fine Riesling Beerenauslese. Alfred Dobson toyed with his food, eating very little.

Marla seemed disappointed that Jack had not taken an active part in the hunt. Salinger had expected she might be despondent from his lack of attention, but she was actually in fine spirits.

She's been using one of the machines, he surmised.

Following a short stroll over the grounds, the men retired to Professor Salinger's library.

"Please join us, ladies," the professor proposed.

"Charlotte and Marla wish to keep me company, George," Nora Salinger insisted, as she led her complaisant companions in the direction of the drawing room.

A subdued George Salinger monitored the exodus with disappointment.

An earthling served Jack, Martin, and Alfred ice-cold glasses of Dom Perignon while the three men lolled comfortably in leather chairs. Professor Salinger searched momentarily for a volume, which he extracted from a shelf.

Rejoining the group, he read a short passage from the book.

"'We hold these truths to be self-evident, that all men are created equal, that they are endowed by their creator with certain unalienable rights, that among these are life, liberty, and the pursuit of happiness.'

"What do you think of that statement, Alfred?" the professor asked.

"Those are some of the most noble words ever penned by a human hand," Dobson said.

"Yes, how fitting your assessment is, Alfred. The words are stirring, as you say noble. But the words and the beautiful sentence they have formed simply happen not to be true. No body of human beings has ever been created equal in the history of the world."

"Remember, Dobson," Martin interjected, "Jefferson was a slave holder who had a penchant for begetting half-breeds on the sultry body of an African beauty, one Sally Hemings. When he penned that sentence, Jefferson was writing for a very restricted body of equals—white male slave owners."

"America was never a nation of equals at any point in its history," Jack added.

Dobson rose from his chair and walked to one of the oriel windows extending from the south wall of the room. He stood with his back to the Salingers. He appeared more interested in the grounds outside than what was happening inside the room.

"All human beings must strive for some ideal state of existence," he said. "The ideal of equality and freedom is what Jefferson was aspiring to. He knew as well as anyone how far from that ideal his country would always be."

Dobson turned and sat down in the window seat.

"But a document like the 1776 *Declaration of Independence* can be a rallying cry in the struggle for freedom by oppressed citizens," he said. "The literal truth of Jefferson's declaration was not as important as the power the tract had in motivating your ancestors to cast off the yoke of my country's King George the 3rd."

"But you see, Alfred," Professor Salinger said, "the struggle to achieve that false and impossible ideal of equality for all of our citizens caused most of the pain and suffering America endured as our nation matured. Three hundred years passed before the United States was able to establish the natural aristocracy that had been destined to rule this great land."

Dobson pulled a pipe from his jacket pocket, struck a laser igniter, and casually drew fire into the bowl.

"A government based solely on money, Professor, should not be graced with that fine Greek word, 'aristocracy'," Dobson insisted, pointing the stem of his pipe at George Salinger. "What you have created here in the United States is a petty oligarchy, a 'plutocracy' as you call it yourself. There is nothing noble about your present system of government."

Jack almost burst out laughing, a lingering effect of the Mary J he had smoked before lunch. He recalled with amusement his father's jousting with a pipe the previous evening.

"Absolute power is extremely ennobling," Martin suggested, "except to those who have no power, Dobson."

George Salinger began to tap repeatedly on the text of Jefferson's declaration in the open book lying before him.   ·

"The fallacy in your reasoning, Alfred, is your contention that you would be able to maintain your ideal state of equals, through the goodness of altruistic human behavior, once you achieved it," the professor insisted. "Any political system involving so-called free and equal men and women will self destruct eventually, because of the very differences in ability and aspiration among the constituents that your doctrine of equality attempts to suppress."

Martin Salinger rose from his seat and walked over to the coffee urn. He stretched his body and yawned with animal pleasure. George Salinger scrutinized his first born son with pride.

"Force, absolute unassailable force, is the only stabilizer of any conceivable political system," the professor said. "The destructive rise and fall of nations that are permitted to evolve freely is inevitable, given the absolute fact that human beings are incapable of sustained good will toward others."

"Think of why you have been sent here, Alfred," Martin Salinger said, sipping from his cup. "Think of what has been happening in England in recent years. Your country has experienced the same progressive polarization of the rich and the poor that we experienced in the United States several generations ahead of you. Such polarization is inevitable in a free market capitalistic society. And you know that once such polarization reaches a critical threshold, the less privileged—motivated by envy—always turn on the rich. The same brutal assassinations, the same killings and kidnappings of the children of the privileged, the same pitiless rape of aristocratic women are all occurring in Britain today, just as happened here prior to the establishment of our final solution."

"Terrorism is terrorism, Alfred," Jack added, flashing a look in his father's direction "whether domestic or foreign. And sustained systematic force is the only thing that can root it out and destroy it."

"Our present age of enlightenment, Alfred," the professor continued, ignoring Jack's remark, "was brought into existence when we finally, after 300 long years of ignorance and petty idealism, began to study history, really study history in depth, and learn from the lessons of the past. When we took that critical step, we established the basis of our salvation and the basis of the stabilization of our society.

"During your stay here, Alfred, you and I will discuss in great detail the basic principles necessary to the survival of a stable economically based aristocracy. I know that in the time available to me, I will be able to convince you that plutocracy sustained by absolute force is the only form of government that can possibly endure. Our system, Alfred, will be the first to last at least a thousand years. No system of government has been able to accomplish that, including the Roman Empire. But the United States of America, one nation under Plutus, will achieve that noble goal."

"Professor, Professor," Dobson said in exasperation, "you will never convince me that the enslavement of 99% of your own people was just, or in any way inevitable."

"Your problem, Dobson," Jack said, "is that domestic terrorism in your country has not hit home for you personally. Your family has not been brutalized yet. Terrorism, domestic or foreign, is not rational human behavior and such acts cannot be dealt with using reason. We tried every possible rational solution to stop the escalating violence inflicted upon us, whether the perpetrators were our own citizens or the representatives of foreign ideologies. Nothing worked. In order to ensure our survival, Alfred, we had to simultaneously accomplish a domestic coup and carry out our war in the Middle East. Both actions were necessary and justified."

"We don't blame the earthlings, our former fellow citizens, for their attempts to reverse our inevitable rise to absolute political power, Alfred," Professor Salinger interjected. "In fact, we understand their actions. In their place, we would have done the same. Unfortunately, by the time of Second Independence Day, those Americans who would become the Angel class had simply amassed such a disproportionate amount of the nation's wealth that our natural and complete separation from the masses was a fait accompli, no longer negotiable. The earthlings represented a clear and present danger to our survival. Their enslavement was unavoidable.

"But my dear, Alfred," the professor added. "Why must we dwell so on the negative aspects of our system? Think of the advantages that have accrued to the Angel class since we gained absolute power in America. By reordering the allocation of the economic resources of this great nation, we have created the most secure government that ever existed. We have the strongest military machine in the world. Angels have the highest standard of living of any people in history and are the most educated citizens of any society the world has known. Our medical research program has made significant strides in life extension. And most importantly, Alfred…"

"I know, Professor," Dobson interjected. "Angels pay no taxes."

George Salinger's eyes dissected Dobson's face. He carefully closed the book lying before him on the table.

Jack winced. The professor's body language was unmistakable. He was at the podium. A lecture would follow, formal and didactic. George Salinger was incapable of sustaining simple conversation with other human beings.

"We have no gender or racial bias in our society," the professor continued, as if reluctant to lose his train of thought. "Like the noble Greeks before us, we are tolerant of homosexuality. We have had the wisdom to stop legislating against personal human expression. We have legalized marijuana, cocaine, and the use of virtual eroticism machines for personal gratification, as a necessary complement to stable bonding—bonding no longer plagued by divorce, sexually transmitted diseases, or adultery.

"We have the greatest level of religious toleration the world has ever seen," the professor insisted. "Although—like the ancient Greeks and Romans before us— we make fatuous public displays of our symbolic worship of Plutus, the great God of Wealth, we allow freedom of religion to all, especially to the earthlings. We have capitalized on the fact that religion has always been the opiate of the oppressed and downtrodden. But the belief in a transcendent reality can be of solace to men or women of any intellectual capacity. We do not enforce any system of religious persuasion on anyone. All of the world's religions, from paganism and witchcraft to the highest forms of theology, are represented in the various segments of our society. As long as social order is maintained, our citizens may hold any esoteric opinions they wish.

"Finally," the professor said, "we have slowed the process of technological advance sufficiently to guarantee the future stability of our society. By choice, we have suppressed research and development of alternative energy sources, such as nuclear fusion. Now that we control the vast petroleum reserves of the Middle East, the stability of our society would best be served by continuing worldwide dependence on crude oil."

"In short, we have created heaven on earth, Alfred, a heaven appropriately populated by Angels," the professor dramatically concluded."

Jack thought his father might break into song.

Dobson moved to a seat at the foot of the table, opposite George Salinger. He dropped his lanky form into the chair and sat confronting the professor.

"While those who live below you, your earthlings, have the lowest standard of living of any enslaved people in human history," he said. "No dominant group has ever been so unjust, Professor.

"You do not permit the oppressed citizens of America education and you deny them adequate health care, unless the diseases they are subject to affect Angels adversely. At the same time, you attempt to mollify these so-called earthlings with unlimited quantities of beer and copious doses of the most primitive forms of religious pabulum.

"You realize, of course, that while the life expectancy of Angels has been rising, actuarial projections suggest that the life expectancy of the earthling male in America has fallen below 50 years for the first time since 1900."

"Earthlings live in a free society," Martin Salinger interjected. "We demand services of them, naturally, but we do not impede them in any way from doing exactly as they wish. If they suffer the consequences of the unrestricted behavior we have granted them, that's of little concern to us."

Alfred Dobson sat with his hands in his lap, slowly shaking his head from side to side.

"And so, Martin," he said, looking up disdainfully, "you let them die or suffer the effects of diseases you have the power to eradicate in an instant."

"For someone so concerned with our exploitation of earthlings, Dobson, it seems odd to me that you made excellent use—I am told—of one of our privileged body servants last night," Martin said. "How was Loreena, by the way?"

Dobson reddened with rage and embarrassment. He rose from his chair.

"The fallacy in your system, of course," he said with deliberation, "is the fact that you have sown the seeds of your own destruction by creating subclasses of Angels, Professor Salinger. How did George Orwell express your problem in his prophetic mid 20th century novel? 'All of us Angels are equal, but some of us Angels are more equal than others.' As you admitted when we first spoke, Professor, every Angel has access to luxuries, but only Seraphim have access to political power. In time, disgruntled members of your own class will rise up to destroy you. How do you intend to prevent that?

"And I might add, Professor Salinger, that I have also read your rather inflammatory writings about manifest destiny," Dobson said. "Do you really feel the implications of your position have been lost on your neighbors to the North?"

George Salinger's tone became patronizing. He was obviously losing patience.

"The loyalty of our own subclasses is absolutely beyond question, Alfred, make no mistake about that," he said. "Angels of every subclass have more wealth than they would ever be able to dispose of. The state subsidizes wealth maintenance, the direct opposite of taxation. Every Angel in America has everything any human being could ever want. There is absolutely no basis for discontent. Should one of our privileged citizens become disgruntled despite such largesse, we have implemented appropriate means to rid our society of such malcontents."

As Salinger listened to his father, a perverse thought brought a wry smile to his face. He could not afford an Aphrodite 609.

"And as for our neighbors to the north, as you call them, we have no intention of taking action that would compromise the Canadians in the near future, Alfred," Professor Salinger continued.

"My intention has been simply to point out the greatness of forward looking thinkers from America's past. I wanted our modern intelligentsia to appreciate the masterstroke of our great journalist, John L Sullivan, who first coined the term 'manifest destiny' in 1845. And I wanted to celebrate the accomplishments of two of our greatest presidents. John Tyler gave us Texas. Then James K. Polk, the greater of the two, shrewdly induced your own country, Alfred, to give us the Oregon territory below the 49th parallel, by negotiating a brilliant treaty with England in 1846. Polk then wrested New Mexico and upper California from our neighbors to the south and extended our national borders from sea to shining sea.

"When I think of the accomplishments of these great men, Alfred, I sometimes regret that the presidency has been so weakened in the present era."

Dobson tapped the burnt tobacco from his pipe. Jack watched the shower of ashes falling into the ashtray.

"But your intention, Professor, has clearly been to celebrate the precedent for extending your national borders—as you affirmed so eloquently in your treatise—in the event the *need* should arise again. You Americans have always been bothered by that vast tract of territory that separates Alaska from what you once called the 'lower 48'."

With this scornful final observation, Alfred Dobson rose from his chair and stormed out of the room.

"I think you have your work cut out for you this time, Father," Martin said.

George Salinger smiled vacantly.

"Yes," he said, "I suppose I do."

CHAPTER 16

▼

Despite Nora's efforts, the Saturday evening birthday celebration in Jack's honor did little to relieve the tension at Haworth Manor. Salinger ordered a night flight home after dinner on Sunday, happy to return to his living space in the city.

Fortunately, Dominique Cantrell was not on duty that evening. The pilot was a haughty fourth quintile male, one economic rank higher than most turbo chopper pilots. The flier's reticence was irritating. Salinger suspected the pilot considered himself above the job. Jack waited impatiently until the security force had finished sweeping his living space for evidence of intruders. He was relieved when the patrol finally left.

Salinger was glad to be back home. Martin and the professor had done little to hide their hostility. Then, Marla had insisted on speaking to him privately earlier that afternoon. They met briefly, but uncomfortably, in the library.

Jack recalled the tentative exchange.

"We could call our engagement off, Jack" Marla began. "We're not obligated to go through with this, but you know how disappointed my parents and yours will be if our match doesn't take place."

"My brother's failure to produce the all-important heir seems a feeble excuse for a lifelong match, Marla," Jack said.

"Do you want to announce the breaking of our engagement tonight at dinner?"

"Look, Marla, I'm trying to get used to the idea…Some people in our circumstances manage to fall in love with one another…eventually. I truly hope that happens to you and me."

Marla's face brightened.

"Then you don't want to break it off with me?"

"No," Jack said, stretching the truth. "Just cut me some slack and let's see what happens."

Marla had embraced him. As Jack sensed the sincerity of Marla's affection for him and the suggestiveness with which she pressed her breasts to his chest, a wave of empathy passed over him, together with a momentary twinge of desire. Salinger regretted his indifference to his prospective mate. He kissed Marla with genuine warmth. He then escorted her to his room for cocktails before dinner. They had made love, but the coupling had been perfunctory and mutually dissatisfying. He had left Marla with little, other than his hastily ejaculated seed.

CHAPTER 17

▼

A week passed. Salinger had no further contact with "MP." Sitting at his computer, he fumbled for a capsule of Serenity 400 as he downloaded a copy of *Liberty Leading the People* from the virtual reconstruction of the Louvre in Paris.

Salinger spent several minutes peering at the image of the bare breasted figure of Liberty. He wondered why Miranda Lee-Weston conceived herself in this particular way. Madam President had indicated that she saw Salinger in the painting too. Was he in the vanguard of those living revolutionaries near the head of the charge, or among the dead lying at Liberty's feet?

Salinger needed to talk to someone, if only to hear a human voice and see a human face that was not that of a stranger in need. On several occasions, he sat in the semi-darkness turning Dominique Cantrell's identification card over in his hand. Although electronic communication with Dominique was not strictly illegal, Salinger would be badly censored should anyone find out he was making unprofessional overtures to an Angel of lower economic status. Physical contact was strictly forbidden.

Finally one evening, despite his reservations, he decided to call Dominique.

Salinger studied the connection. The communication was priority one, the highest possible level of security. He flipped on the camera.

Dominique Cantrell was usually wearing a flight helmet during Salinger's contacts with her. When he had interviewed her as part of her application to join his security team, she had worn her hair in dreadlocks. This evening, Dominique was wearing her hair down. Her crystal clear holographic image floated before Salinger's eyes. As he voyeuristically drank in her stunning image in virtual reality,

Salinger realized he had never encountered a woman so beautiful in his life. His own face registered pain, however—delicious, but melancholy pain.

"Hi, Doc," Dominique said. "What a pleasant surprise. I didn't think you were going to call."

Salinger's hesitancy betrayed the awkwardness of the situation. He hardly knew what to say now that he had initiated personal contact with Dominique Cantrell.

"I guess I'm feeling a little gloomy," he confessed. "A classic case of the therapist in need of some help himself."

"Hey, I was a little down too," she said. "After all, it's been over a week since I gave you my card! Maybe we can cheer each other up, Doc."

"You could start by calling me, Jack."

From that point, a floodgate seemed to open between the two. They bantered for nearly two hours, yet the time seemed like minutes to Salinger.

Dominique insisted on hearing more about his encounter with "Madam President." Salinger was not able to level with her about the affair.

"Like I told you," he lied, "'MP' was just another imaginative drug seeker. I haven't heard anything more from her."

When he casually mentioned Alfred Dobson's sabbatical at Haworth Manor, Dominique seemed inordinately interested.

"I've always been fascinated by English men," she explained.

Jack said little about Dobson's political views despite Dominique's insistence in hearing all about him.

"You're making me jealous," Salinger confessed.

"Don't be silly."

"So tell me about your life," he said, changing the subject.

"In your visual module, you see the most ambitious person in America," Dominique said, laughing, but serious.

"I love flying, but my real passion is law enforcement. I'm applying for an entry-level spot at the Department of Homeland Security, but the application is a back breaker. I may finish it before my hair turns grey."

The two shared a great deal more that evening than either had anticipated. Salinger used the exchange with Dominique to unburden himself.

"I wish I could change everything," he said. "I think about leaving here and trying to do something with my life. I didn't choose medicine. I'm a lousy psychiatrist, Dominique. Sometimes I think about joining an earthling settlement and practicing there. You know…basic medicine.

"But then I have to admit my incompetence. I'm being dishonest with myself. And so I'm left with an unhealthy dose of self-loathing."

Dominique Cantrell was a sympathetic listener.

By the time the conversation finally came to an end, Jack Salinger was more captivated by her than ever.

"I really enjoyed this," he confessed, before signing off for the night.

"Me too," she said.

"Would you be upset if I called you again?"

"More so, if you didn't, Jack."

"So where are we going with this?"

"Where do you want to go with me?" Dominique asked.

"Have you ever thought about doing something absolutely stupid and ill-advised?"

"Only since I met you, I'm afraid."

"Are you serious? I mean really serious?"

"The prospect of becoming involved with you excites me, Jack Salinger," Dominique said. "But we both know the risks. I need to be certain you won't hurt me. Getting to that point will take some time."

"Maybe we can just see how things evolve," he suggested.

Dominique leaned closer to the video monitor and her holographic image implanted a kiss in virtual space.

Salinger sat with his fingers pressed to the spot where her lips had been, long after Dominique's image had faded into nothingness.

Over the ensuing days, Jack and Dominique spent hours talking about everything and nothing. The level of flirtation gradually intensified. Then one night, the interaction progressed to telecommunication sex.

She had bathed and shampooed her hair just before he called.

"I'm a mess," she said. "Give me a minute to get presentable."

"I've never seen anyone so beautiful," he admitted. "Please, don't change a thing."

Dominique shied before the camera, the way extremely beautiful women sometimes do when caught in a situation where they feel less than their best. She was wearing no makeup. Her natural beauty was even more stunning than her slightly more composed appearance in public.

"Let me look at you," Jack pleaded.

Dominique peered into the monitor, drinking in Salinger's unqualified adoration. After a moment's hesitation, she slipped out of her robe. Salinger asked

Dominique to tone down the lighting in her living space. Against the soft background illumination, her virtual image floated in space before Salinger's eyes.

He activated his electronic tactile probe and teasingly guided the beam over Dominique's body while the camera lens zoomed in and out on the striking features of her anatomy. She was far more beautiful than Salinger had imagined. He deftly caressed her breasts with his intrusive virtual probe, massaging her nipples with his circle of tactile brightness. The stimulation was soon too intense to bear. With a frustrated gasp, Dominique reached over to her control panel and reluctantly aborted the session.

After several additional interludes of frustrating mutual visual and tactile exploration, Dominique insisted on an open-ended grace period with no further contact. She needed some space, she said, to sort things out. She had not expected a response to Salinger of such intensity, she confessed.

"I'm afraid, Jack, of what might happen to us," Dominique added. "This started out as a lark, but it's evolved into something much bigger than I thought it would. I'm going to ask that I not be assigned to your flights for a while."

"I'm upset, Dominique, but I'll respect your feelings," Salinger said. "I won't try to contact you, but I hope you'll change your mind and call me."

CHAPTER 18

▼

Salinger began to drink more heavily following the break with Dominique. He intensified his exercise program when his weight started to edge up, but the wearisome repetitions became increasingly tedious.

Then Salinger received another CD-ROM from Miranda Lee-Weston.

Recalling the uncomfortable exchange with his father, Jack was convinced destruction of the package was his best option. In fact, he did not break the seal on the container for several hours.

Salinger returned to the Museum of Computer History. Faces there appeared furtive, challenging. He followed his contact back to the location of the old PC. The president's operative seemed more reserved than she had been on the previous occasion. Or did the prickly sensation at the back of his neck betray paranoia affecting him alone?

This time the message was terce. President Lee-Weston wanted to meet with him covertly at a location to be disclosed later. He was given two access code numbers to a web site that would exist in cyberspace for a span of exactly three minutes on the following Tuesday evening. One of the numbers would signal his agreement, the other his refusal to meet with the president. Should he activate the abort sequence or enter no input at all, he was informed he would not be contacted again.

CHAPTER 19

▼

Salinger sat at his desk trying to outline his options on a palm top. He had digitally entered a few lines of tentative input. Suddenly, he pitched the unit at the wall. Components scattered across the floor.

He tried to analyze his reactions to Miranda Lee-Weston. On a primitive level he acknowledged simple ego gratification and curiosity about the president's bizarre plan to "certify" the sitting government of the United States. But there were subtleties too—the titillation of danger, for example, and the reemergence of all of his repressed youthful feelings about the injustices of the current political system. Most important, Jack knew he would relish any change in American society that would permit his unimpeded pursuit of Dominique Cantrell.

Salinger ambled over to his refrigeration unit and retrieved a cold beer. He held the bottle to an overhead light and watched a swirl of tiny bubbles moving mindlessly through a liquid world. There was no reason to debate these issues. He knew he really had no options. Against the exciting possibilities of defying his father and of making a difference with his life, he saw the mediocrity of a future bonded with Marla LaBaron. He saw, too, the grinding boredom of the years ahead, engaged in a stultifying profession that had also been chosen for him.

Salinger rose to his feet and began to shadow box through his living space. He could feel the tension leaving his body as he parried about the room. He shot a series of merciless jabs into the empty space before him, following up with two murderous rights that staggered his imaginary opponent. He stood over his vanquished adversary, taunting him, screaming declarations of victory into the bloodied face.

That Tuesday evening, Jack Salinger punched in his acceptance of the president's invitation and crossed the threshold into the unknown.

CHAPTER 20

▼

Salinger could see little below the aircraft, as the chopper passed swiftly through the night sky. He could not believe this was happening. He was being transported to a rendezvous with the President of the United States, or was he?

He could see his body strapped in its seat, as if he were watching from another part of the aircraft. He wanted to make his way to the seat next to that image of himself and shake some sense into someone who could not possibly be him.

Salinger realized he might be on the way to a secret place of interrogation by agents of the Department of Homeland Security, or even on the way to a swift execution. He would learn very soon whether he was to be a patriot in the cause of freedom, or a traitor to his country.

Salinger peered at his own avatar. The person he saw may not have been cut out for political activism. That person, he knew, might at heart be an abject coward. Perhaps he *was* no Salinger, as his father constantly reminded him. His earlier participation in protest politics may have been a sham. The threat of execution had unmanned the political activist he had tried to become. That threat had driven him to groveling cooperation with his demeaning reeducation program. Who then was this person peering into the dark nothingness outside the window of a military helicopter on this night of uncertainty and potential danger? What was he—Jack Salinger—doing here?

Salinger had been dressed in full camouflage during his escorted trip to the heliport, in order to conceal his identity from operatives of the Department of Homeland Security. The president had assured him during her last transmission that he was undoubtedly already under surveillance. His father's questions seemed to confirm that Mrs. Lee Weston was correct. The bulky uniform had added to the theatricality of the situation.

The crew of the chopper had fed Salinger's paranoia further by greeting him at the heliport with disturbing silence. He had tried to identify a Presidential Seal on the aircraft, but found no markings of any kind. His several attempts at making small talk had also been ignored.

Salinger bit down on his lower lip and dried his hands—yet again—on the knees of his fatigues.

Once on the ground, Salinger was led over some rough terrain into a bunker dug into the side of a hill. He was directed into a room and unceremoniously shown a seat at a conference table. Two other men and one woman were present. Salinger thought he recognized one of them from an American Psychiatric Association meeting he had attended several years ago. Salinger's confreres seemed no happier to be here than he was. In the next several minutes, six additional people, four women and two men, were led into the conference room, filling the empty chairs around the table.

Then, with no fanfare or announcement, she simply entered the room, accompanied by two heavily armed marine colonels in full combat array. With the others, Salinger snapped to his feet and saluted Miranda Lee-Weston, President of the United States.

She had that overwhelming charisma characteristic of many U.S. Presidents. Salinger was certain Lincoln had had it. He had read that John F. Kennedy, Ronald Reagan, Andrea Rellinger, and William Jefferson Clinton had been graced with an aura that enabled them to command any room they entered. Miranda Lee-Weston had that kind of magnetism. Her presence was far more engaging than any holograph Salinger had seen. She was obviously no puppet, but a strong charismatic leader. Salinger thought of *Liberty Leading the People*. He sensed he would follow Miranda Lee-Weston to the ramparts on his hands and knees. Before the president had spoken a single word, Salinger knew his life was about to change.

"Ladies and gentlemen," she began, after taking her place at the head of the table. "In the interest of your own security, I am not going to ask you to introduce yourselves. I know you have mixed feelings about being here tonight. I salute your courage and your dedication to your country's welfare. You should all be very proud…"

President Lee-Weston paused and scanned the faces of her guests. When she turned her attention to Salinger, he was unable to take his eyes from the president's face. That same sadness he had observed on the monitor screen was visible, but even more striking this evening was Miranda Lee-Weston's resolve.

"I have explained in part why I have called you together," President Lee-Weston continued. "A reasonable question I'm sure many of you have is why you were personally asked to participate. All of you are psychiatrists, certified by the American Board of Psychiatry. Each of you was involved in some way in liberal politics earlier in your careers, some overtly, others only covertly. As far as I have been able to ascertain, none of you have a life partner. None of you have children."

President Lee-Weston paused briefly.

"None of the women here tonight are pregnant to my knowledge. If that is not the case, please speak up."

The five females glanced at one another, but no one spoke.

The president continued.

"You are among 56 potential signatories from the so-called Angel class of a document I will present to you in detail later this evening called *The Certification of America*. Before you leave this compound, I'm going to ask each of you to sign the original certificate, which has been transcribed onto parchment.

"As I suggested during our previous communications, the *Certification of America* will become a symbolic call to arms for the 2nd American Revolutionary War. Should you agree to become signatories, your lives will never be the same. You will be taking an irreversible step into history. There will be no turning back.

"In order to convince you that rebellion against the existing government is absolutely necessary, there are some things I need to show you. We will be away from this room for approximately two hours. Please feel free to refresh yourselves in any way you need. If at any time you decide you do not wish to participate, you will be escorted back to your living spaces. No evidence of your attendance tonight will exist. If and when you are ready to proceed, please join me outside."

The attendees rose en masse and saluted as the president left the room. Salinger surveyed the faces of his compatriots. There was no need to speak. He could read in those faces what the others were reading in his. So this was not a game. Miranda Lee-Weston was in deadly earnest about what each had assumed was either an elaborate practical joke or sheer madness, the "certification" of the present government of the United States as no longer competent to rule by reason of insanity.

But Salinger could also read in the faces of the others that same veneration of the president that he was feeling, that same overwhelming response to her charisma, her dedication, and her resolve. Salinger wondered what the others were seeing in his face. He tried to peel layer after layer of discontent, boredom, and cowardice from that face so those staring at him could compare his image favorably with that of the president's. Out of the nebulous unreality of the scene, a great sense of patriotism and pride emerged. Salinger forcefully walked outside to join President Lee-Weston, anxious to learn where on earth she could possibly be taking him.

CHAPTER 21

▼

The party left the compound in a convoy of three heavily guarded military transport vehicles. Salinger had never seen earthlings in full military uniform before. The polished young men and women in the Special Forces unit accompanying President Lee-Weston did not have the deferential expressions on their faces characteristic of the earthlings he had known at Haworth Manor.

Salinger looked into the face of a heavily armed earthling commando. The young woman maintained resolute eye contact with him. Salinger turned his eyes away.

He wondered how many such troops President Lee-Weston had under her command.

The silhouettes of dimly lit buildings gradually emerged from the shadows, the village illuminated indistinctly by the light of a low hanging moon. The carriers pulled to a halt in what Salinger assumed was an earthling village. Muted interior lighting illuminated a few of the buildings. The streets were empty except for a few skulking dogs that surveyed the intruders with suspicion and then moved on.

President Lee-Weston led the group to a structure that resembled an assembly hall. Inside, several people were watching the state run television network on an antiquated 35" TV screen. The visitors milled about, not knowing what to expect.

Miranda Lee-Weston greeted one of the earthlings with familiarity and then returned with the man to the group of awaiting Angels.

"I would like to introduce Mr. Robert Carlson," the president said. "Mr. Carlson is a resident of this community. He has graciously agreed to be our guide during our tour of inspection. Please feel free to direct any questions you might have to Mr. Carlson at any time."

The outdated title of respect that President Lee-Weston had used sounded strange directed to an earthling. The members of the lower class were usually addressed by given names alone.

The group followed the commander-in-chief and Mr. Carlson out onto the street. Carlson led the visitors to one of the houses located in a cul-de-sac a block and a half from the assembly building. The president's honor guard took up positions in the street as the rest of the group crowded inside the dwelling.

Salinger surveyed the small one room house. The furnishings were plain, but functional. There appeared to be no electricity. The light was coming from several tallow candles. Some dried vegetables and what appeared to be the smoked carcasses of small animals were suspended from the ceiling in the kitchen area. A bed, with a partially hidden chamber pot beneath, was visible behind a drape in one corner of the room. The curious faces of two children were peering down at the group from a loft, the small girl and boy alternatively giggling and then punching one another in the ribs to be quiet. A woman, who appeared significantly younger than Robert Carlson, stood demurely near the far wall. Except for an occasional furtive glance at the group, she was staring at the floor and seemed mortified to have her living space invaded by strangers. Salinger noted the absence of books, any kind of telecommunication device, or a television set.

"Mr. Carlson is employed at a collective farm six miles from here," the president explained. "He walks to and from work, unless he is lucky enough to hitch a ride. We Angels provide the Carlsons with a monthly subsistence level allotment of bread and beer. As you know, earthlings are not allowed access to firearms, but they are permitted to trap animals and raise some livestock. Mrs. Carlson manages the household and the family vegetable plot in the village commons. She is Mr. Carlson's fourth wife. Can you tell the group about your first three wives, Mr. Carlson?"

Robert Carlson rose to his full height. He stood surveying the group defiantly, his eyes fixed angrily on each of his visitors in turn as he spoke.

"The first was taken from me by the field boss at the farm," he said. "She chose to stay with the man when I tried to get her back. The next two died having them," he added, jerking his finger toward the children above his head.

"Where were the children born, Mr. Carlson?" Miranda Lee-Weston asked.

"There in that bed."

"Who delivered them?" the president asked.

"The village midwife helped with the first, but I delivered the second one myself. She couldn't get here in time."

"I suppose your first wives died of child bed fever?" one of the women asked.

"I suppose that was why," Carlson said.

"Have you had other children?" Salinger asked.

"Nine—all dead, but these two."

"Infection killed the children too?" another one of the physicians inferred.

"No," Robert Carlson said heatedly. "You people killed every one of them!"

"Mr. Carlson is actually quite well off," President Lee-Weston suggested, breaking the momentary uncomfortable silence. "He has a stable job and has been able to afford to purchase four mates. Many of his fellow citizens can never accomplish even a single match. Would you introduce the children now, Mr. Carlson?"

Robert Carlson reached up to the loft and extracted the two youngsters in turn, placing them on the floor before the group. The little boy immediately assumed a squatting position on his haunches. Salinger noticed that the boy's skin was inky blue. Instinctively, he reached down and looked at the child's fingernails. As he suspected, the ends the fingers were clubbed and knobby. The child obviously had congenital heart disease and was not oxygenating his blood properly.

"How old is he?" Salinger asked, looking into the boy's youngish face.

"He's 14 years old," Robert Carlson said.

The little girl sat on the floor with a terrified expression on her face. She searched the room for her stepmother and then lunged in the young woman's direction. The girl was obviously paralyzed from the waist down and dragged her lower body across the floor.

"She has had poliomyelitis, a disease your profession once called infantile paralysis," Miranda Lee-Weston explained. "As you know, Doctors, Angel children are immunized against this infection. Supplies of the vaccine for earthling children tend to be—shall we say—limited. I suspect none of you has seen a case before."

At the invitation of President Lee-Weston, Robert Carlson spoke briefly to the visitors gathered in his home.

"I have things good, compared to some," he began. "But there is no where for me to go from here, but to my grave. I get by. My wife and children will not starve during the coming winter. The village magistrate and the local militia will keep the lawless in the hills outside at bay. But I want something more from this life. I don't want the course of the years ahead to be etched in stone like they are. That's what you Angels have taken from me. The possibility of another life, any other life than the one you have decided I will lead. I'm willing to fight you to the death for the power to determine my own future."

Both of Carlson's fists clenched tightly as they hung at the sides of his robust frame.

"And there are many more like me," he said.

The second stop on the president's tour was the office of the local village law enforcer and magistrate, John Mitchell.

Mitchell was a burly man in late middle age with a full beard. He lived alone in a garret above his office, which also contained a single holding cell.

"I wonder if you would describe the rule of law in your community, Mr. Mitchell?" Miranda Lee-Weston asked.

"Not much law, per se," Mitchell responded. "We have to enforce rules of conduct in order to survive. I see to that."

He nodded in Robert Carlson's direction.

"I get help, of course, from some of my fellow citizens from time to time. We basically have zero tolerance, an old legal term used years ago in the days before Second Independence Day, for malfeasance of any kind," Mitchell elaborated. "A good many folk seem to feel it's proper to take advantage of the young and helpless. We see to it that such offenders stay out of our territory, or we round them up and deal with them."

"Do you conduct trials of any kind for these offenders?" the president asked.

"I suppose you could say we do," Mitchell responded. "But, we don't waste any time. The penalty for misconduct is hanging."

"For any offense?" one of the visitors asked.

"For most," Mitchell acknowledged. "We deliver the more incorrigible offenders to the owners of the larger Angel estates. For a consideration," he added arrogantly.

"I'm surprised such hardened criminals are accepted as indentured servants," one of the physicians suggested.

Salinger did not betray his embarrassment, as he recalled the recent hunting party outside Haworth Manor.

"They're not used as indentured servants, Ma'am," Mitchell said. "The Angels help us process these hard cases, is all."

Salinger was glad Mitchell did not elaborate. Perhaps he was only being paranoid, but he felt President Lee-Weston scrutinizing his face with somewhat heightened interest.

"How are you paid for your services, Mr. Mitchell?" Miranda Lee-Weston asked.

"I get a modest stipend from the state. I pay no rent on my humble abode," he said. "I'm also provided with firearms and ammunition. Otherwise, I live on what comes my way. The pipeline of the black market smugglers can always be tapped when necessary."

Mitchell was delighted when the president asked him to show the group his arsenal of firearms. The weapons were secured in a trunk under lock and key. As a certified officer of the law, John Mitchell was authorized a sidearm, a high powered rifle, and a double-barreled shotgun. He was issued ammunition only in exchange for cartridges or shotgun shells he had expended. Other than regional peace officers like Mitchell, earthlings were not permitted to own firearms.

"Of course, we have a group we like to call scavengers, who have managed to get their hands on firearms," Mitchell said. "Most of them are body strippers who kill for pure pleasure and for whatever they can get off a corpse. The majority of them prey on city folk, but now and then one will come our way."

"We have to be extremely vigilant," Mitchell added.

"You said you live alone, Mr. Mitchell," one of the women said. "The advantages of your position would suggest you could afford to have a wife."

"I could, Ma'am," Mitchell responded. "But people in my position live under fairly constant threat of assassination from the stray scavengers who pass through, or from other malcontents, as you might suspect. I never thought it would be fair to have anybody dependent on me. Besides, I have opportunities bonded men like Carlson here don't have. I've never felt the need of permanent female companionship."

"Female prisoners are afforded special treatment then?"

Mitchell's burly face reddened briefly.

"Well, like I said, Ma'am, we hang most of the offenders, but we don't hang all of them."

Leaving the magistrate's office, Salinger and the others followed Robert Carlson through the darkened streets of the village, and then along a path that led out into the countryside. Some distance from the settlement, the group reached what appeared to be an abandoned warehouse.

The air inside the building was stale and rancid. Row after row of cots filled the interior space. Here and there gowned figures moved among the beds carrying lanterns and casting slowly moving shadows along the walls.

The group was offered protective masks made of crude pieces of cloth. Salinger was not certain how effective they might be. He noticed that President Lee-Weston chose not to wear one. Salinger, like a few of the other physicians, also deferred. He knew the gesture was pure presumption.

Jason Burleigh, the village doctor, greeted the president and her entourage.

As Dr. Burleigh's eyes bore into the group of Angel physicians, his disdain was palpable. He was here only because Miranda Lee-Weston had asked him to participate.

Burleigh led the president and the assemblage of physicians from bed to bed, inviting them to suggest a diagnosis from time to time. Salinger was disconcerted at how fascinating the sufferers were to the group. All of the physicians had been exposed to training in general medicine and surgery prior to specializing in emotional disorders. The visitors were acting like an eager band of third year medical students. Salinger knew in his heart, he was not the only one of the crowd who regretted he did not have a portable diagnostic scanner. He looked with envy at the primitive stethoscope hanging from Dr. Burleigh's neck, but he could not bring himself to ask the doctor to allow him to borrow the instrument.

Many of the old diseases were represented.

A young woman was in the advanced stages of consumption, the diagnosis obvious from the crusted blood that flecked her lips.

Smudge pots were burning at the sides of another bed. President Lee-Weston bent to the woman's ear and whispered to her for a moment or two. Then she drew back the blanket the "patient" was draped with. A foul smelling, weeping ulcer had replaced the woman's right breast. Salinger had once seen an individual with this advanced stage of breast cancer in a collection of medieval miniatures depicting the maladies of the flesh.

A young man lay in one of the cots. He had obviously sustained a fall. Both of his lower limbs were deformed by incompletely reduced fractures. He was paralyzed from the waist down.

"Why are these people here?" one of the physicians asked. "Wouldn't they be more comfortable at home?"

"In order to die comfortably at home, Doctor," Dr. Burleigh said with poorly disguised irony, "one must have a home. This place is a common ward for the incurably ill or dying. Most of the inmates were carried here by their family members and abandoned to their fate. Fortunately, a far greater number of our people do care for their ill or dying relatives at home. Guilt makes those not capable of such altruism share a modicum of food with the patients and the staff. The village also provides support from the proceeds of a primitive system of local taxation."

A compendium of disorders, all of them morbidly fascinating, was on display.

Some of the cots were fitted with openings to accommodate those with chronic colitis or dysentery. The stench around these beds was unbearable.

Some of the patient's bodies were grotesquely deformed by collections of fluid in the abdomen or legs. The physicians sorted these out as caused by advanced dropsy, liver failure, or the unchecked spread of abdominal cancers.

Many of the patients had what the earthlings called "slim," an old African term for the sexually transmitted infection, HIV, a disorder rare enough to be reportable in the Angel community.

Dr. Burleigh led the group out of hearing of the patients. He looked at the president as if debating what to say next. The dark scowl on his face left no doubt of his frustration with the proceedings.

"You must realize, Doctors," he said, literally spitting the title through his teeth, "how many of the conditions we have seen here tonight are treatable. Your government sees fit to withhold adequate medical supplies from practitioners like me. My major source of drugs is our primitive black market.

"Since I cannot obtain sufficient quantities of medications to effect long term cures, I try not to dispense false hope…

"President Lee-Weston urged me not to say this…But, I must ask how you can live with yourselves?"

Burleigh stopped speaking. His eyes, aflame with anger, swept the group standing abjectly before him.

"I have patients to see," he said, his voice ringing with sarcasm. He turned and stormed off to the far side of the clinic.

The sobered group of Angels broke up and began to wander aimlessly among the beds, speaking to the patients. Salinger, like the others, was trying to recover his self-esteem. Dr. Burleigh was one of many American physicians not wealthy enough to have been declared an Angel on Second Independence Day.

Several gowned women moved among the group offering what solace they could in a health facility with little available therapy. Amulets, rosaries, crucifixes, a single menorah, and other religious icons were attached to the walls at the head of each bed.

Suddenly, Salinger caught a glimpse of the face of one of the nurses. The woman turned from him abruptly and walked away, but he caught up with her. He turned her face to the dim flickering light. He could not believe his eyes.

"Heloise, is that you?" he said in shocked disbelief.

The familiar face had been ravished by time and was scarred by a plethora of purple red nodules interspersed with deep scars, which the woman tried desperately to hide behind a shawl. The lesions were consistent with a severe case of smallpox, or worse, the ravages of secondary syphilis. Heloise had been Jack Salinger's nursemaid when he was a boy. They had been together until he was seven and she was fourteen.

"You've changed greatly since I saw you last, young Jack, but I could never forget those eyes I once loved so much," she said tearfully. "I tried to see if it might be you without having you recognize me."

"But they told me you'd died, Heloise…years ago," Salinger said.

President Lee-Weston and the others were standing a few feet away, monitoring the exchange.

"No, Jack, I didn't die, but many times I wish I had."

"How did you get here?' he asked, still astounded.

"I was taken from you when I reached a proper age for…other functions," she said. "I served your father and then later your older brother. Martin was his name, was it not? Eventually, I was put out."

Salinger was dumbfounded and also bitterly ashamed that the others were hearing this. He could not drive the image of his other former earthling friend, Loreena, from his mind.

"My people did not welcome me back with joy," Heloise said. "I was traded from man to man until I became sick, with this," she said, indicating her face. "At least when I lost my attractiveness, the men began to leave me alone."

Salinger turned to the president, his voice seething with frustration and rage.

"I have to do something for this woman," he said. "And for the others here," he added with a sweep of his hand.

"But you know as well as I, Doctor, that any covert assistance of earthlings by members of our class is considered treason against the state," President Lee-Weston said, her voice ringing with irony. "As you know, the crime is punishable by death."

"I don't care about that," Salinger said.

"Well then, Dr. Jack," the president said, being careful not to reveal his surname to the other members of the group. "You will shortly learn that there is—in fact—a great deal that you can do for these people."

CHAPTER 22

▼

Robert Carlson led the group back into the center of the village. The president insisted on a brief stop at a church that abutted the main square. The building smelled of must and stale sweat. Two candles were burning at either side of a nondescript altar. A man and two women were chanting in a pew near the front. The sound was low and droning, impossible to decipher. Salinger was reminded of plainsong, Gregorian chant, or the mantras of Tibetan monks.

President Lee-Weston knelt for a moment in one of the pews. The group of physicians milled about uncomfortably, as if debating whether to join her. Fortunately, the president defused the situation by regaining her feet and leading the group outside. She chose not to comment or offer any explanation for the visit.

The last stop on the tour was located about 20 minutes away by convoy. As the trucks pulled to a halt, buildings were visible in the pale light of a now fully risen gibbous moon. The structures appeared to be bombed out shells, shadowy forms silhouetted against the moonlit sky.

"We will not be here long," President Lee-Weston said. "There is really nothing to see. In this area, an attempt was made to bring down a military helicopter with a primitive surface-to-air missile. The missile missed its target. In response to the attempt, however, a retaliatory bombing raid was conducted against the village that once stood here.

"627 men, women, and children were killed here in less than an hour. When were you last confronted by the charred remains of a 4-year-old child?"

Salinger recalled the intensity in Dominique Cantrell's voice as she called in the GPS coordinates from the turbo-chopper that Friday afternoon a few weeks ago. He tried to convince himself that the village could not possibly be located so close to Haworth Manor.

The entourage was subdued during the ride back to the staging compound. When they had collected in the conference room, the president spoke again briefly.

"I would like to reemphasize what Dr. Burleigh told us," she said "Most of the medical and surgical conditions we observed this evening are treatable or controllable. No Angel in America need be concerned about such disorders. The officials of our present government are very proud of the fact that Angels have the highest quality medical care in the world.

"We did not address the conditions that afflict earthlings not sick enough to be confined to bed. The old nutritional diseases—pellagra, rickets, and scurvy—afflict many of these people, especially the children. I know you are also well aware that sexually transmitted diseases are rampant in the community. That's why you take such precautions to ensure the health and safety of those earthlings you call privileged, those who live—for a time in any event—as indentured servants at your family estates.

"Mr Carlson, our guide, selected his fourth wife because she appeared to be disease free. He performed a pre-nuptial examination as crude as the evaluation one might make when purchasing a horse. You know far better than I do, Doctors, that she may be infected with HIV 2,3, or 4. For that matter, Mr Carlson himself may have been infected with HIV by one of his former wives. The state has seen fit to withhold protective devices…

"Our magistrate, John Mitchell, has also been playing that old game called Russian roulette with the—shall we say—fringe benefits of his employment."

Miranda Lee-Weston rose from her chair and began to pace at the head of the table as she continued speaking.

"We are responsible for the egregious living conditions of the so-called earthlings living among us. You've seen tonight what passes for health care in these villages. The state has also seen fit to deny earthlings formal education. These communities labor under an equally primitive system of law and order, and—far worse—earthlings have no opportunity to better themselves in any way. I'm certain the rage in Mr. Carlson's voice about that latter point was not lost on any of you.

"And yet, life in these villages is far superior to conditions existing in our surviving cities. I did not take you to one of them because of concerns for your safety and because a group of this size would trigger a response from the security forces of the sitting government. You would learn much, however, should any of you living in one of these places ever make a descent to the streets.

"Sadly, human beings revert to a state of bestiality if the constraints of civilization are removed from them. Our remaining American cities have become veritable jungles. We should display warnings, advising those who enter to abandon all hope. Life in our American cities, for earthlings, has become far worse than anything we might encounter in Dante's hell."

The president paused briefly, surveying in turn the sober faces of the men and women quietly listening.

"I wonder why we have permitted these things to happen here in the United States of America," Mrs. Lee-Weston continued. "The usual excuse is that we had no choice. The Council of Twelve would have us believe that the Angel class rose to power because of the natural tendency of humankind to evolve an aristocracy based on elitism, in our case economic elitism. The Council of Twelve also has an absolute stranglehold on our society, you will rightly say, backed by ruthless military power. What can any of us do? I suppose similar reasoning brought some solace to the Germans who once lived under the shadow of the Gestapo during the Third Reich.

"I have devoted my presidency, ladies and gentlemen, to the rectification of the wrongs that exist in our country. I have spent the last six years, using silence, deception, and cunning as my implements, laying the groundwork for what will shortly take place in these United States. I believe my cause is just and were I not to act at this time, I would be in violation of my sacred honor.

Miranda Lee-Weston seemed embarrassed by the formality of her last words. She paused, and stood for a moment peering into the faces of the men and women in her audience.

"After a short break, we will reconvene in this room," the president said finally. "As I alluded earlier, I need to recruit 56 signatories to a document I will show you this evening. As you will recall, 56 brave citizens appended their signatures to the 1776 *Declaration of Independence*. None of you are under any obligation to sign *The Certification of America*. Should you consent, however, your signature will become affixed to the document this very evening.

"As you know—to its great credit—the Council of Twelve has been rebuilding our former national capital in Washington, D.C. The work has been ongoing these past 24 years since Second Independence Day. We will complete that noble task. When we reestablish the National Archives Exhibition Hall, the original *Certification of America* in parchment, with the signatures of some of you in this room tonight, will be displayed beside a reconstructed replica of the now lost 1776 *Declaration of Independence.*

"*The Certification of America* will be a call to arms, ladies and gentlemen. The value of the statement will be highly symbolic, since many of the people to whom it will be directed have been deprived of the basic education necessary to comprehend it.

"Earthlings, to their credit, have been conducting schools in their homes and villages. They have tried to maintain the literacy they enjoyed prior to Second Independence Day. Now that the libraries and booksellers in their territories have been closed, however, the only reading material available to them are the few volumes they managed to save from the book burnings of two and a half decades ago. The elder generation has tried hard to sustain interest in literature among the young, but they are fighting a losing battle. The greatest damage we have done to our so-called earthlings has been to poison their desire to learn to read.

"Many of the recipients of *The Certification of America* will not be able to read it themselves, but the document will be read to them in the assembly halls, on the farms and factories, and in the streets. The literal contents of the certificate are actually not that important, but the symbolic value will be of mythic proportions, almost beyond calculation.

"When you leave here, tonight, there will be no record that this meeting took place. All of you have the option of contacting the Department of Homeland Security and reporting what occurred here this evening. I am hoping that what you have seen tonight will at least persuade each of you to remain passive in this regard.

"You should know that for years, I have been under suspicion by the director of the Department of Homeland Security. My late husband, Ambassador Weston, died for the cause I am asking you to join. I have been under constant surveillance. Director Striker may be aware that I am here tonight. He and I are engaged in a deadly game, my will and my resolve versus his. One of us will win and one of us will lose the battle we are engaged in. There will be no stalemate. So far, Commander Striker has chosen to give me considerable latitude. I suspect he has an agenda of his own. It remains to be seen whether he or I will prevail."

Miranda Lee-Weston stopped speaking and began to walk toward the door. The group of physicians rose to their feet and stood at attention until the president had left the room. Salinger knew that everyone present craved an opportunity to talk the situation out at length. Before there was time, an officer entered the room and ordered the physicians to disband. The group was informed that they would reconvene in this same room after a short break.

CHAPTER 23

▼

The group had been escorted outside for fresh air. The president's military personnel discouraged open conversation by the attendees, for "reasons of security." When the twelve psychiatrists reconvened in the conference room, electronic facsimiles of the *Certification of America* had been placed on the table before each chair. Two officers in full battle uniform stood at either end of the room, doubtless to maintain order and discourage discussion. The hour was now well past midnight.

Jack Salinger read his copy of the president's declaration at least four times. He scrolled back to the top of the drafted document and read it again.

"The Certification of America

When in the Course of Human events, it becomes necessary for the people of any nation to dissolve the government set above them, a decent respect to the opinions of humankind requires that they should declare the causes which impel them to take such action.

We hold these truths to be self-evident, *that not all human beings are created equal,* but that *all human beings must be afforded certain unalienable rights.* Among these are Life, Liberty, and the pursuit of Happiness. Governments are established among People, but governments must derive their just powers from the consent of the governed. Whenever any form of government becomes destructive of these ends, it is the right of the people to alter or abolish it, and to institute a new government. When a long train of abuses evinces a design to reduce them under absolute despotism, it is their right, it is their duty, to throw off such government and to provide new assurances of their future security.

Such has been the patient sufferance of a whole body of human beings disparagingly designated *earthlings* and *Angels* and such is now the necessity which constrains them to alter their present system of government. The history of the governing body of these United States, designating itself the COUNCIL OF TWELVE, is a history of repeated injuries and abuses, all having in direct object the establishment of an absolute tyranny over these United States. We herein attest that the corruption pursuant upon the acquisition of absolute power by said Council of Twelve, has deprived the Ministers of said Council of all semblance of human reason. We attest that every action taken by said Council of Twelve from an arbitrary date titled Second Independence Day proves beyond the shadow of a doubt depravity of mind in said Ministers consistent with loss of reason; to wit, insanity. To prove this, let the following Facts be submitted to a candid world.

The Council of Twelve has reestablished the obscene institution of human slavery in these United States. We certify that no group of rational human beings conducting the business of government while enjoying unimpeded use of human reason could possibly take such a regressive step in human affairs unless said group were suffering from collective and hopeless delusions.

The Council of Twelve has withheld education, basic shelter, the rule of law, and adequate health care from those human beings designated by them *earthlings*. We certify that such action constitutes premeditated genocide, an action not possible of commission by persons in full possession of human reason, and therefore also the action of a body of humans beings collectively and criminally insane.

The Council of Twelve has instituted restrictive policies affecting members of the so-called class of *Angels*; these policies have deprived Angels of the right of free choice in the pursuit of human social interaction. Such acts constitute enslavement in the name of freedom, a delusion consistent with grossly aberrant thinking.

The Council of Twelve, while professing liberal toleration of all religious beliefs, has in fact substituted money, in the personification of a false god known as Plutus, as the reigning deity in these United States. We certify such behavior indicative of a delusion afflicting the governing body of this land, consistent with a bona fide diagnosis of destructive and collective psychosis.

In many broadcasts, tracts, and publications, the Council of Twelve has professed that all citizens of these United States, whether Angel or earthling, are absolutely free. We profess that all citizens of these United States have been in fact enslaved, whether physically or ideologically. Therefore the professions of the Council of Twelve are patently delusional and represent the collective misconceptions of a group of persons laboring under the impairment of mental illness.

In consequence of these facts and opinions, we the undersigned, fully trained in the profession of psychiatry and endorsed by the American Board of Psychiatry, do hereby certify the present governing body of these United States to be hopelessly and irremediably insane. We certify the Council of Twelve no longer mentally competent to carry out the business of governing.

All citizens of these United States, whether designated *Angel* or *earthling*, are hereby absolved of any allegiance to the sitting governing body of this land, so certified to be incompetent to govern by reason of insanity. We urge all citizens to rise up in rebellion aimed at the complete overthrow of the Council of Twelve and all of its instruments of power.

We urge immediate restitution of the 1787 Constitution of the United States of America and all instruments of power established therein.

For the support of this *Certification of America*, with a firm reliance on the justice of our actions, we mutually pledge to each other our lives, our fortunes, and our sacred honor."

Salinger stopped reading and surveyed his colleagues. Several were still poring over the document. Most of the psychiatrists had completed their examination of the certification and were sitting with their eyes straight ahead, as if preoccupied with the significance of the president's tract. Salinger made eye contact with one of the men. That individual made a swirling gesture at the side of his head with his index finger leaving little doubt of his assessment of Miranda Lee-Weston's proposal.

Salinger tried to analyze the situation as objectively as possible. Madam Lee-Weston was seething with poorly suppressed rage, that much was clear. Whether she was psychotic or not was a more complicated question. Salinger was debating that critical issue when the president reentered the room.

She asked the psychiatrists to remain in their seats. She took the chair at the head of the table. She was carrying a laptop computer and a parchment scroll.

"I apologize that security concerns have made it necessary to restrain open discussion of my proposal until now," Mrs. Lee-Weston began. "Please confine disclosure of your identities to given names only.

"I would like to begin by showing you a series of holographs."

Miranda Lee-Weston activated an imaging module connected to her computer.

Horrifying images from the bombed village materialized in virtual space. Salinger could feel the president's eyes boring into him as the holographs sequenced. When he made momentary eye contact with Madam Lee-Weston, he had little doubt the village was the one near Haworth Manor.

The president next displayed a series of holographic images of earthling children.

"You see no hope in these faces, am I right?" the president asked.

The expressions on the faces were apathetic and devoid of any enthusiasm for life.

"We have robbed these young people of the will to achieve," the president said. "And these young people are not *earthlings*, my friends, they are our compatriots and they represent the future of America. We must give them something to believe in."

Miranda Lee-Weston placed her hands on the table and leaned toward the group.

"I would be most grateful to have your signatures on the certification, ladies and gentlemen, directly below my own," the president said. "I feel it is only fair, however, to point out that the cost to each of you personally will probably be enormous, should you decide to sign the document. Your families will also be endangered, by agents of the Director of Homeland Security and—in some cases—by operatives of my own who have already infiltrated your family estates."

Mrs. Lee-Weston was looking directly into Salinger's eyes as she finished her statement. He recalled the vehemence of Alfred Dobson's criticism of the political system Jack's father had designed.

"So you're asking us to betray our families as well as our country, Madam President," said one of the women, who identified herself as "Justine."

"I'm asking you to make monumental sacrifices to save your country, Justine," the president replied.

"Madam President," Salinger said, "would you permit me to ask you a rather personal question? I took the liberty of looking into your background—very informally, of course—and I could find no justification for radical activism in your social or educational history. How did a person with your conservative upbringing become so involved in radical leftist politics?"

The president reached for a glass of water.

"I've always been a student of history," President Lee-Weston responded, "since my undergraduate days at Smith. The deepening polarization between the rich and poor in our country, a polarization that began to accelerate at a logarithmic pace during the early decades of the 21st century has always represented—for me—a tragic, but fascinating period in our nation's history.

"I don't think the conservative occupants of the White House during that pivotal period were evil men and women. Perhaps some of the demagogues whose media transcripts I have studied could be considered so, but the promotion of personal and corporate wealth was genuinely felt to be in the best interests of the country. Without question, however, the flagrant support of monied interests through lobbyists and political action committees represented the selling out of democracy and fostered the evolution of a wealth-based aristocracy. But neither of these terms—'lobbyist' or 'political action committee'—can be found anywhere in the original United States Constitution."

A man called Martin had been waiting for an opportunity to interject. Salinger studied "Martin" closely. The name and the individual's demeanor resonated unfavorably.

"These instruments of political activism that you disparage, Madam President, were necessary foils to an apathetic constituency with the worst voting record in history," Martin said. "There was no democracy in America that could be 'sold out,' as you put it."

Salinger watched in fascination as the president's fists clenched and her knuckles whitened.

"When the nation found justification—on whatever basis, Martin—for abandoning the weak, the poor, and the homeless, the principles of humanism and democracy were lost, destroyed on the twin shoals of self-interest and greed. When those in power allowed millions of men, women, and children to go without adequate health care, the groundwork for the enslavement of the underprivileged was established and the present dismal state of affairs was foreordained."

Martin's face reddened as he leaned toward Madam Lee-Weston.

"What other solution could there have been to the reign of domestic terror our underprivileged—as you call them, Madam President—rained down upon those of us at the top of the economic order?" Martin protested.

Another one of the women—"Kelly"—joined in.

"How can you, as a woman and politician, justify the assassination of America's second female president in such a brutal and merciless way before the eyes of a classroom full of school children, Mrs. Lee-Weston? Was that act of egregious violence a valid protest against the disproportionate accumulation of wealth?"

The president settled back into her chair.

"The questions you raise are difficult to answer. But I envision a political system that would have avoided excesses by extremists at either pole of the economic spectrum, had the necessary reforms been enacted. Such a system, in my view, is the only possible alternative to the present plutocracy."

"What alternative to the present system are you proposing, Madam President?" Martin asked, his tone ringing with sarcasm.

A smile passed over Miranda Lee-Weston's face.

"Well, to misquote one of my favorite passages from *The Second Part of King Henry VI*, 'The first thing we do, Martin, is make certain the trial lawyers never rise from the dead.'"

Martin scoffed.

"One of the most important reforms Professor George Salinger introduced was the abolishment of frivolous lawsuits by Angels," the president said, glancing briefly at Salinger. "Earthlings, under the present system, have no recourse to any redress by the law, of course.

"But seriously, our reestablished Congress must pass ironclad laws to ensure that rampant litigation does not gain a foothold in our reformed society. We must establish a National Board of Arbitration to settle civil disputes, but an operative principle of our reforms in this area must include a healthy degree of individual responsibility for accidents or other adverse events. I am in agreement with George Salinger on this issue.

"But I differ strikingly from Professor Salinger's position about intention in relation to criminal acts. The Council of Twelve's legal code recognizes no gradation of culpability whatsoever. Any crime in our nation is punishable by death. The Council claims this Draconian policy is absolutely necessary, in the interest of social stability. I disagree most vehemently. We have to take intention into account in matters of law again. In a just society, there must be degrees of culpability, even in cases of murder."

As Salinger listened to the president's impassioned, but rambling remarks he had to question her emotional stability. He sensed others at the table entertained similar feelings.

"But let me continue," the president insisted.

"I'm sure that all of you noticed that *The Certification of America* clearly proclaims that not all human beings are created equal. Jefferson's assumption of equality, even if he did not really believe the concept to be true, *did* get us into considerable difficulties, as Professor Salinger has so eloquently pointed out.

"We cannot have a viable system of government that does not recognize the fact that our citizens, while they must be equal under the law, are simply not equal in most other respects. Those who are more intelligent and more creative than others will always struggle to assert their individuality, accomplish more, and acquire more than their fellows, unless they are enslaved like our friend, Mr. Carlson. This is a simple, but profound fact of life."

The president raised her hands, palms up, in acknowledgement of the exclusivity of the group. Several of the psychiatrists shifted uncomfortably in their chairs.

"Inequality among Americans—as epitomized by the growing disparity in the accumulation of wealth—became increasingly obvious and had increasing consequences at the turn of the 21st century," the president continued. "A cap on runaway, out of control, capitalism was necessary. Such a cap could have prevented the tragic events that occurred during the first half of the 21st century, but this was impossible to legislate. Our final Congresses were hamstrung by gridlock and could not stop the momentum that eventually led to a state of egregious economic inequality.

"The obscene disparity between compensations of CEOs and entry-level employees in corporate America at the beginning of the 21st century, to say nothing of the absurd compensation afforded entertainers and professional athletes, was only the beginning of a process that was carried far beyond any conception of rationality or justice."

"But if Congress—assuming that body was resurrected, which I doubt will ever happen—*did* legislate salary caps, what would motivate people to take on the responsibilities of a CEO, say?" Justine asked.

"I like to know what your benchmark maximum salary would be," a man identifying himself as "Jeffery" added.

"Well, Jeffery," the president said, "in a restored American democracy, I would suggest that the position of elected President of the United States should rightly be considered the most important job in the nation. Congress could set the president's salary at any value felt to be fair compensation, considering the importance of the position. That salary would be the highest individual remuneration in the land. No one else would be legally able to earn more.

"And as for motivation, Justine, power and influence have always been powerful incentives in the past."

Martin laughed out loud.

"The president's proposal doesn't sound all that bad to me," Salinger suggested, "especially if the chief executive's salary was high enough to serve as a reasonable yardstick."

"Give me a break, Doctor!" Martin scoffed. "As an Angel with your head in the clouds, you can make any self-effacing statement you want. But I suspect you would balk as much as anyone at a substantial reduction of your present income."

Salinger reddened under Martin's assault, but he could not refute the truth of the man's remark.

Mrs. Lee-Weston checked her chronometer.

"The document I would like you to sign tonight also declares that every human being must be afforded the rights to life, liberty, and the pursuit of happiness," she said. "That statement implies rights to adequate housing, health care, education, and law and order. In my opinion, these things can best be assured under a limited form of socialism.

"My solution to the problems that destroyed the first American Republic is to mandate a society that optimally combines limited socialism and controlled capitalism, a society that will bring the greatest happiness to the greatest number of people."

"So you would substitute out of control taxation for out of control capitalism, Madam President," Kelly said. "I don't find anything encouraging in that kind of solution."

"We both know taxation is necessary, Kelly, except in a state as elitist as the one we are living in today. We both also know that taxation in America—when it existed—was usually progressive. In fact, the top 5% of the population, economically speaking, did pay the majority of taxes at the turn of the 21st century. One can hardly blame the wealthy for utilizing every possible measure to reduce their burden of taxation.

"We can't fault individual Americans of talent and enterprise who felt justified in trying to accumulate as much wealth and avoid as many taxes as possible during those crucial early decades of the last century.

"But the economic elite at the turn of the 21st century should have realized that unchecked polarization between the rich and poor invariably leads to class warfare and to the eventual destruction of any society that allows such a state of affairs to evolve. I believe Lincoln once said that republics are usually destroyed from within.

"The most privileged citizens of that era were simply not perceptive enough to foresee the inevitability of class warfare based upon the economic policies of the leadership of the nation. That class warfare, when it came, was responsible for the eventual destruction of American democracy.

"If the citizens of any nation are unable to see the consequences of egregious self-interest, that nation is doomed to self-destruction. But I believe that enlightened Americans living in a restored democracy will have learned from the past and will have sufficient vision to make the individual sacrifices necessary to collective survival. If such is not the case, I believe all humankind may be fated for extinction."

"I'm very much afraid you may be correct, Madam President," said "Adrian".

Miranda Lee-Weston acknowledged Adrian's comment. Her voice softened.

"Reform in so many areas was possible at the turn of the 21st century," she said, sadly. "I find it tragic that nothing was done to turn the tide, until men like George Salinger suggested the present system of government in America, a system rife with inherent injustice for the majority of our citizens.

"But we are now in a position to wipe the slate clean and start over again. We are in a position to recreate a reformed American democracy. We can correct the mistakes made by our predecessors. We must seize the opportunity to accomplish this great goal."

Salinger was painfully aware that several in her audience had stopped listening to the president, but Madam Lee-Weston continued to outline her vision.

"We must return to the principals of the original American Constitution, but we must ban special interests and political action committees. We must have a simple and equitable system of taxation with ironclad proscriptions against loopholes and other forms of injustice. We need to resurrect public television and the Internet, but we have to liberate these educational tools from the obscene commercialism that destroyed them at an earlier time in our history. We must foster a system that will allow qualified candidates to run for political office and be heard on a nationalized communications network without the influence of monetary contributions by large corporations or wealthy individuals. We must nationalize America's health care, housing, transportation, and communications industries.

"We must establish a national work force that will provide honorable employment in exchange for financial assistance.

"We must also allow talented people more assets and more income than those less aggressive than they, but we must place an ironclad cap on the unchecked accumulation of individual or corporate wealth.

"I think that with a completely fresh start we can construct an equitable system that will be viable in America. I would like to see controlled capitalism and limited socialism in this country serve as the model for a system of global government. An effective global executive and legislative body—a United Nations no longer stymied by the power of the veto—would be able to ensure basic human needs to all people on this planet by capping the obscene accumulation of wealth by a minority corrupted by greed. Such a form of global government is ultimately our only hope for survival."

Martin, Justine, and a few others sat shaking their heads in disagreement. The president seemed unperturbed.

"When I was a student at Harvard Virtual Law School," she continued, "I loved to read Mr. Justice Oliver Wendell Holmes. I'd like to paraphrase one of my favorite passages for you, ladies and gentlemen.

"I do not pin my dreams for the future to my country or even my race. I think it probable that civilization somehow will last as long as I care to look ahead. I think it not improbable that humankind, like the grub that prepares a chamber for the winged thing it never has seen but is to be, may have cosmic destinies that we don't yet understand.'

"Then, Justice Holmes describes how he watched the streetlights come on as he was walking one evening in our former National Capitol. He describes the streetlights first as 'evil eggs' from which he feared the 'new masters of the sky' would come, those who will bring us to ruin.

"Holmes goes on. 'But then I remembered the faith that I partly have expressed, faith in a universe not measured by our fears, a universe that has thought and more than thought inside of it, and as I gazed, after the sunset and above the electric lights, there shone the stars.'"

Miranda Lee-Weston stopped speaking. She sat searching the faces of her audience for some response to the vision of the future she had just proposed.

"Madam President," Justine said, "with all due respect, your proposals—admirable as they may be in theory—seem simplistic, idealistic, and perhaps not even anchored in reality. Do you really think people are going to respond to this document of yours? Fomenting a nation wide revolution seems to me an impossible task in the times we are living through.

"Let me be blunt. Have you considered that many rational people, none of them psychiatrists, would certify your proposals more insane than any actions the Council of Twelve has taken?"

The president stared into Justine's eyes with an expression of great patience on her face. For the first time that evening, Salinger was aware of how tired she appeared to be.

"Do you think a radical change in the present government of the United States is necessary, based on anything you have felt in the past, or on anything you have seen tonight?" she asked, extending the question to the others.

Salinger thought about Dominique Cantrell, among many other things.

"Yes, I'd like to see changes, Madam President," Jeffery said. "But my problem is simply this. I don't think you can possibly succeed."

"You know, Doctor, there is an old adage that I find useful in circumstances like these. It reads: 'Never underestimate your adversary'. The Council of Twelve and the Department of Homeland Security have underestimated me. They have underestimated my resolve, and that of the people I represent."

Salinger was struck by the president's choice of the word "represent." She was an appointed official. She did not represent the common people, she represented the Council of Twelve.

Miranda Lee-Weston quickly outlined her immediate plans.

"During my second term in office, I have been carefully reading the mood of the people. You recall, of course, the anger expressed by Mr. Carlson earlier this evening. Similar discontent is also rampant in the lower economic divisions of the so-called Angel class. I have been slowly recruiting partisans to my cause. I believe that history is on my side, ladies and gentlemen. We have a seething cauldron of rage in this country that needs only a spark to set off an immense, nationwide explosion in support of radical reform. *The Certification of America* will be that spark.

"As a first step, millions of copies of *The Certification of America* will be released nationwide, electronically and in hard copy. The document will incite civil unrest, including protest marches and work stoppages. At the height of the resulting disruption, assassins will begin to eliminate the ministers of the Council of Twelve. As unfortunate as such events may be, the success of these assaults will arouse the passions and expectations of earthlings and Angels across the country. Many of these disgruntled citizens will come over to our side, bringing military equipment with them.

"Our growing army of rebellion will next seize the majority of the nation's ammunition depots, military bases, transportation hubs, and media centers. Finally, the insurrection will end in a coup that will topple the current regime.

"We have the full backing and assistance of the British Secret Service and key elements in the British government. My husband worked diligently to establish these connections during his ambassadorship to England. Suspicions of him by operatives of our Department of Homeland Security led to his assassination.

"You will recall how invaluable the British were during our Middle East Campaign. Britain has also been secretly funding my own covert operations for over five years. The British operatives I have recruited see a sort of poetic beauty in the role they will be asked to play during the 2nd American Revolutionary War.

"Perhaps without intending to do so, the imminent Professor Salinger has played into our hands. His increasingly virulent diatribes about manifest destiny have convinced key officials in Ottawa that Canadian national sovereignty is threatened. They have been working tirelessly to garner support for our struggle. Elements of the Canadian Air Force will breach our northern no-fly zone at key locations and provide crucial air support during the final stages of our operation.

"So you see, Doctors, we have allies; we are funded; we are resolved; and we are prepared to take action very soon."

Salinger leaned toward Miranda Lee-Weston. He fought an overwhelming impulse to take her hands in his.

"But surely, Madam President, you are at great risk of betrayal by one or more of your own operatives," he said. "You have also exposed yourself to those of us present at this meeting. How can you be certain that the director of Homeland Security is not aware of your every move?"

"As I said earlier, Commander Striker and I are involved in a very intricate game. I realize Striker is aware of a great deal of what I am doing. But you don't know Kurt Striker. He is a man as angry about certain aspects of our current system as Mr. Carlson. Striker has an elaborate agenda of his own. He and I will engage each other relentlessly, knowing full well that only one of us will ultimately prevail. Let's just say that it is not in Kurt Striker's own interests to stop the rebellion too soon."

"Why is that, Madam President?" Kelly asked

"Because Kurt Striker is trying to consolidate enough power to accomplish a coup of his own."

An uncomfortable silence followed the president's last remark. Salinger surveyed the faces of his colleagues. The emotions he was able to read were mixed, but sadness was the predominant mood. The president rose from her chair. The group of psychiatrists followed suit.

"We will disband now and I will meet with each of you individually," the president said. "The identities of those who sign the certification will not be immediately disclosed."

After Mrs. Lee-Weston left the conference room, the psychiatrists were escorted individually to a personal rendezvous with the president.

"Well, Dr. Salinger, have you decided to sign the document?" Mrs. Lee-Weston asked when she entered the room to which he had been taken. "Because of your close relationship to one of the creative minds behind the present system of government in America, I would be most grateful to have your signature as the very first on the certificate, directly below my own."

"Can I ask you something?" he said. "That village…the one that was bombed. Was that settlement near my family's estate?"

"I'm afraid it was," the president responded.

Salinger sat looking at the parchment scroll the president had unrolled and the antique fountain pen she was holding out to him. He was weighing some sobering possibilities. Miranda Lee-Weston might be afflicted with manic depressive dysphoria caused by unresolved grief stemming from the death of her husband. She might be suffering from delusions of grandeur. The president might be frankly psychotic. He had to admit that his own psychological stability could be seriously questioned.

And yet, Salinger felt certain Miranda Lee-Weston would find her signatories somewhere. He felt, too, that her cause was just. In the end, his feelings for Dominique Cantrell decided the issue.

Is that always the case? Do we always make momentous decisions for purely selfish reasons?

Jack Salinger wanted to think himself a better human being than that. He wanted to share Miranda Lee-Weston's heroism, even if—in the end—that heroism had a tragic outcome.

Salinger thought about the humiliation he had suffered at the hands of his father and his brother. He knew the president's pen in his hand would feel like a lance. With it he could lacerate the heart of a father who had never offered him the slightest hint of love.

He thought about the children in the village, about the earthlings he had met this evening, about his old nursemaid, and especially about some imagined future life with Dominique Cantrell.

He reached for the president's fountain pen, scrutinized the scroll of parchment unfurled before him, and then signed his name below Miranda Lee-Weston's own boldly transcribed signature.

CHAPTER 24

▼

"Grandpa!" a delighted voice cried out, as a small boy ran in the direction of a smiling older man with closely cropped gray hair and a glint of welcoming joy in his eyes.

With a single sweeping motion, the man's arms reached out, picked up the exuberant youngster, and swung the squealing little boy into the air.

"Edward!" the man said, "I'm so glad to see you, my lad."

Kurt Striker tousled his grandson's hair and began to wrestle with an aggressive opponent on the floor of his office. He was soon knocked to the ground and utterly defeated.

Five-year-old Edward Striker soon tired of the game and began the methodical disorganization of his grandfather's desk. Striker smiled at his daughter-in-law, Ilene, as he rose from the floor and reached out to embrace her.

The interlude with his grandson and Edward's wife displaced the rancor Striker was still feeling after his last communication with George Salinger. Striker was under orders to report frequently to the council leadership, but Professor Salinger insisted on personal progress reports concerning his son, Jack. The demand was symptomatic of the professor's arrogant presumption and inflated self-esteem.

"Your son has made two trips to the Museum of Computer History, my lord. We know that on the second occasion he was taken to a location in the administrative section of the facility. The Angel who escorted him to that area has provided little hard information, despite our intensive pharmaceutically assisted interrogation.

"Clearly, the president is using primitive 21st century PCs as a secure means of communication. As I informed the council earlier, my operatives have examined the devices carefully. In each case, the hard drives have been removed. Consequently, our investigations have turned up little useful information."

Striker also knew that Jack Salinger was the individual from his residence building who had boarded a helicopter using unauthorized stealth technology one evening during the previous week. Striker opted to withhold this additional information from George Salinger—for the time being.

"I'm going to urge the council to authorize the president's arrest for pharmaceutical interrogation," George Salinger said.

"Again, I wouldn't be so hasty, my lord," Striker countered. "I still think we should let Mrs. Lee-Weston play her game a while longer."

"I'm not sure the council will agree," Salinger snapped.

"I am at your service, of course, my lord."

"If you uncover any solid evidence incriminating my son, I expect you to take action, immediately! Do I make myself perfectly clear, Commander Striker?"

"Of course, my lord. I have Dr. Salinger under constant surveillance."

Striker found George Salinger's callous disregard for the welfare of his own flesh and blood increasingly sickening. Striker planned to contact the council chairwoman later that day to urge restraint. If ordered to apprehend Mrs. Lee-Weston, he had already decided that certain temporary impediments to her arrest would have to arise.

Kurt Striker turned toward his desk, assumed a threatening lumbering gait, and began to engage in a mock sword fight with young Edward, to the youngster's obvious delight. When stabbed in the heart, Striker grasped his chest and fell theatrically to the floor, dragging his grandson into an affectionate embrace.

CHAPTER 25

▼

Salinger was sitting in his living space in the darkness, listening to the *Adagio* of Tomaso Albinoni. His stomach felt like a ball of knotted rope. The music was doing little to soothe his frayed nerve endings.

He rose from his chair, sauntered to the window, and stood with his finger tips outspread against the glass. At any moment he felt his body might be driven through the pane and hurled into the blackness of space.

Why had he signed *The Certification of America*?

There was no way to contact Miranda Lee-Weston. There was no way to renege, to retrieve his signature, or to reverse the step he had rashly taken. As the president had said, there was no turning back.

Salinger tried to sort through his options yet again. He could contact the Department of Homeland Security. Jack's father had always spoken favorably of the current director, Kurt Striker. Professor Salinger had advised his youngest son not to antagonize Striker, however.

"Kurt, unlike his immediate predecessor," the professor had warned, "will not cut you any slack. I think he secretly holds Seraphim in disdain."

Salinger realized he could expect little sympathy from Kurt Striker. Unless the Department of Homeland Security could find some use for an abject coward and turncoat.

Salinger knew he should also contact his family. All of his instincts told him his family should come first, that everyone's family should always come first, that he owed his family steadfast loyalty. Even the thought of betraying them was nauseating.

Salinger curled his fingers and dragged his nails along the glass. He heard nothing but the plaintive tones of the background music. The ripping screeching sound he anticipated—like that of a buzz saw slicing into his brain—did not materialize.

His family…

All of his life, Jack had stood in Martin's shadow. He recalled the patient he had treated a short time before—Reaves or Reese, was the man's name—who was outraged by the policies of primogeniture and entailment. Salinger wanted to attribute Martin's supremacy to primacy in birth order alone, but he knew better. In every respect that meant anything to the professor, Martin had simply bested a lesser man.

Salinger hammered the windowpane softly with the side of his hand.

Why had he never been able to stand up to his father's overbearing conviction of intellectual and moral superiority? Jack recalled greeting his mother at the entryway to Haworth Manor during the weekend of his birthday celebration.

"Father is right about most things," he had told his mother.

Salinger realized how much he resented his father's pompous self-righteousness. For the second time in his life, Jack Salinger had taken independent action about an issue of great personal importance to him. This time, however, he knew his family would not bail him out if anything went wrong.

Salinger was convinced his family was in no danger on his account. Were he to be arrested, his father would find a way to protect the family's interests.

But then, Jack had to consider Alfred Dobson. Mrs. Lee-Weston had implied that Dobson was a British operative. If he warned his father and brother about Dobson, Jack would be compromising the president and her mission.

Salinger looked at the darkened streets below. An occasional dimly flickering fire provided the only illumination. There were no streetlights, no neon logos. There was no loom in the sky above him. There was no moon. There was nothing but gloom, descending like a stifling blanket from the starless sky.

He turned and sauntered over to the countertop. He removed the caps from the salt and pepper containers and slowly trickled the contents onto the countertop until he had produced two pyramids, one white, one dark. He sat peering at the small mounds.

Salinger watched his detached persona approach Alfred Dobson, remove the weapon from the Englishman's hand, and do what? Save his brother and his father? Or carry out the British agent's mission?

Salinger leaned toward the countertop and blew both of the pyramids away.

The intense pathos of the music was moving and sad. As he allowed the slowly falling notes to mingle with his uneasiness, Jack Salinger saw himself writhing in anguish, impaled on the horns of a formidable dilemma.

CHAPTER 26

▼

Almost a week passed. Salinger was maxed out on Serenity 400s. The psychotropic effects, bolstered by the Mary Js he was smoking, were causing vague hallucinations. Security forces materialized out of the darkness. Salinger was arrested, flayed, burned at the stake. Then, unexpectedly, he received a call from Dominique Cantrell.

"Hey, sweet Jack," she said affectionately. "How have you been?"

Salinger was overjoyed to hear Dominique's voice, but he was hesitant to express his elation openly.

"I've been reliving the sorrows of young Werther," he said. "Unrequited love, you know, can have a tragic outcome."

"Is that by Goethe?"

"Yeah. Have you read any of the old German romances?"

"I recognized the title," Dominique admitted.

"When a desirable woman withholds her love, a man sometimes pines away of a broken heart."

"Poor baby."

"I'm glad you called, Dominique. Hell, some day you may even tell me why you did."

"Do you remember when you asked me if I ever thought about doing something ill-advised and stupid?"

"I seem to recall asking you that."

"That's all I've been thinking about since we last spoke."

"Me, too," he said, realizing the statement was hardly true.

"So let's do something ill-advised and stupid," Dominique said.

Salinger could hardly contain his elation.

"What did you have in mind?" he asked.

"I thought we could fly away somewhere together, somewhere out in the country and have a...maybe a picnic. I'll supply the aircraft, you supply the lunch."

"I suppose I don't have to tell you how much I'd like that?"

"Why don't you tell me anyway?"

"I'd love to go somewhere with you, Major Cantrell."

"Well then, Dr. Salinger, meet me at your heliport tomorrow at 2 P.M."

Everything about the meeting with Dominique was risky, beginning with the unescorted trip on foot up to the heliport. The flight itself was reckless, crazy, a dizzy rush into the unknown. Dominique finessed the chopper's control stick, taking the aircraft into sweeping arcs from side to side; the graceful movement of the machine through the sky became an aerial dance at the raw edges of control.

Dominique giggled as she recklessly piloted the chopper through the air. Salinger strained against the G-forces.

"I wish you could love me as much as you love flying," he said into his helmet microphone.

"I plan to love you more," she said, drawing back on the stick and taking the chopper into another dizzy sweep into the open sky that knotted Salinger's stomach with visceral pleasure.

They passed over the last few settlements and then continued on for nearly an hour until no evidence of human habitation remained below them. Dominique set the chopper down on a grassy plain next to a meandering river.

Dominique activated an intrusion alarm in a 360° arc at a distance of 2 miles from the landing site. She and Salinger set up a nylon pavilion and then took a walk along the bank of the stream. The gentle rush of the flowing water had a mesmerizing, soothing effect. They sat together on the bank holding hands like a couple of teenagers drinking one another in, not saying anything. Finally, they kissed for the first time.

Salinger had never had an experience so exquisite. After a few more minutes of increasingly provocative exploration, he rose to his feet and led Dominique back to the pavilion. Part way back, the alarm sounded on Dominique's security monitor. She activated a thermal scanner. She and Salinger watched the image of a grazing deer cautiously moving through the intrusion zone.

"Not much danger there," Salinger remarked, as they watched the tentative movements of the animal on the screen.

"Not as much as may lie ahead," Dominique said.

They reached the pavilion and Salinger began to set up the picnic lunch he had packed.

"Could we wait on that until later?" Dominique asked.

Many times in the coming weeks, Jack Salinger would try to relive what had happened over the next couple of hours, in his imagination and in his dreams. He had experienced what he thought had been the limits of human sexuality in the past, with the machines, with Loreena. Nothing compared to the time he and Dominique Cantrell spent that day along the river. When he tried to analyze the immeasurable difference between his experience that day and anything that had happened to him before, he could only conclude that they had not merely had sex. He had made love to Dominique Cantrell. He had made love to a woman for the first time in his life. And she had responded with equal intensity and feeling. The sadness of that fact would resonate like a tolling bell in the weeks ahead.

Salinger had fallen asleep. He awoke to find Dominique dressed. She was sitting with her knees against her chest. He noted at once that her makeup was streaked.

"What's wrong?" he said in sudden alarm.

"We have to go," she said abruptly.

"Why, Dominique?" he demanded. "You seemed to be as happy with me as I was with you."

"Look, Jack, I know this sounds crazy, but we just have to leave."

He dressed silently. They packed their gear and walked back to the helicopter. Jack tried to get Dominique to open up on the flight back to the city, but she remained non-communicative.

When he deplaned at the heliport, she lifted off without saying anything. Again, he could read pain in her eyes. Salinger gained little solace from his conviction that Dominique Cantrell was as emotionally upset about what had happened as he was.

During the next few days, Salinger bombarded Dominique's telecommunications station with messages, pleading with her to return his calls, but she did not respond. He could not imagine what had gone wrong. His experience with her had been the most intensely satisfying of his life. She had seemed as deeply involved with him.

After several days, Salinger finally stopped trying to reach Dominique. He was convinced he would not see her again.

CHAPTER 27

▼

Following the breakup with Dominique, Salinger crashed. Before long, his practice was in trouble. He began to cancel sessions. The thought of himself as a physician was repugnant. Contacts with his web site remained high, but Salinger became increasingly confrontational with neurotic Angels.

Then, late one afternoon, Salinger received an unexpected log on.

"Charlotte?"

"Jack, you've got to help me! I don't know what to do."

Charlotte Salinger was calling from her portable telecommunication module. The visual feed was not high quality, but she appeared to be in a shopping pod outside the manor. From time to time, Charlotte's eyes darted suspiciously into the crowd of Angels milling about in the background.

"What is it, Charlotte. What's wrong?"

"I don't even know where to begin, Jack. Maybe I shouldn't be bothering you..."

"Don't disconnect, Charlotte. Just start at the beginning."

"I keep a paper journal, Jack. I've been doing that for years. I think Martin has been looking at it. I've been so stupid, Jack. There are things in it..."

"How can you be sure he's been doing that?"

"When I made my last entry...I remember exactly how the book was positioned. It's been moved, Jack, I know it has."

Charlotte was nervously fiddling with the visual scanner.

"Charlotte, how can you be so sure?"

"I'm so damned compulsive, Jack. I always keep my things just so."

"You said there are things in it...in the journal."

"Martin…Well, you know how much trouble we've had…with the babies."

"Yes…Please, Charlotte, go on."

"Martin never wanted anyone to know this, but when we were tested his counts were very low. They didn't exactly say he was sterile, but the doctors told him he would have trouble…

"Oh Jack, I'm so scared."

"But you became pregnant, Charlotte."

"We tried hard for over a year…but nothing happened. There was this boy, Jack. An earthling…He had not yet been sterilized. I…I used him, Jack, both times."

"And you wrote about that…in your journal?"

"I know how stupid that must sound."

Salinger placed his virtual hand on Charlotte's.

"We've been trying again…Martin and I. But nothing has happened. Last week, I wrote that I was thinking of asking you to help me."

"What do you mean, Charlotte?"

"I was going to ask you to help me get pregnant, Jack."

"And you think Martin may know that?"

"I'm sure he knows, Jack. I'm sure he knows everything. You know him, Jack. You know what he'll do."

"Charlotte, I'm going to contact your family. You must go to them, immediately."

"I can't jeopardize them, Jack. I'm going away, somewhere Martin will never find me. Please…I need you to help me. Will you give me temporary access to your expense account?"

"Of course, Charlotte. But you can't deal with this alone. Let me send a security unit to pick you up. We can work this out together."

"Your living space will be the first place Martin will look for me, Jack. Please, just give me the access code."

Salinger transmitted the information. After Charlotte had disconnected, he redialed her number several times. There was no answer. He peered into the empty space Charlotte's image had occupied long after her holograph had slowly faded away.

CHAPTER 28

▼

Following Charlotte's log on, Salinger made a series of urgent, but increasingly frustrating calls.

Nora Salinger informed Jack that Charlotte was away, visiting her family in Newport. Jack insisted that his mother call him immediately when Charlotte returned to Haworth Manor.

The Cordells were evasive when Jack called. Charlotte was not with them, they said. Salinger related his concern for Charlotte's welfare and advised her father to file a missing person report if Charlotte did not contact them within 24 hours. The fact that the Cordells were noncommittal, left Salinger with some hope that Charlotte's parents knew something they could not, or would not, disclose.

The anticipated contact from Martin did not happen.

No withdrawals were made from Jack's personal expense account.

He debated informing the authorities about Charlotte's situation himself, but he didn't want to compromise his sister-in-law's chances of a successful flight. He was left with a sense of foreboding, made worse because there was nothing more he could do for Charlotte.

CHAPTER 29

▼

Release of *The Certification of America* was now imminent.

Using old spamming technology, facsimiles of the certificate would be uploaded to as many computers as possible in a single nationwide electronic mailing within the Angel community.

Small hard copies of the document were the key to the success of the rebellion. Once the final signature had been collected on the original, the certificate had been scanned onto CD-ROM discs. The electronic image had been set up for hard copy reproduction using print shop software on turn of the century computers collected and sequestered in storage warehouses during President Lee-Weston's second term.

Once he was identified as a signatory, Salinger would have to go underground. A helicopter escort would be sent for him. He would join President Lee-Weston and the other signatories at a secret command post.

"In case of untoward circumstances," the president had warned, "you will have to leave your living space and make your way over ground to a safe house in your sector."

Salinger was given the coordinates of the new refuge, which replaced those of his previously assigned location. A ground transport escort would pick him up at this new rendezvous point, in case air evacuation was not possible.

Salinger retrieved his emergency pack and reprogrammed the GPS homing device with the lat/long coordinates of the new safe house. He tested his head and body armor for proper fit. Then he broke down, cleaned, and reassembled his firearm, a 19th generation Glock automatic, with silencer and full lethal as well as stunning capacity.

Salinger tested the heft of the Glock. He assumed a series of firing positions and directed a hail of imaginary bullets at equally imaginary assailants.

Could the president's plan work?

Salinger visualized couriers surreptitiously moving through the earthling territories with facsimiles of the document secreted on their persons. Clandestine public readings would take place. In factories, farms, assembly halls, churches, and village squares all over America, literate earthlings would read copies of the certificate to attentive audiences. The information would incubate and simmer for several weeks, but finally earthlings and many sympathetic Angels would begin to respond to President Lee-Weston's call to arms.

All of this *could* happen.

The rebellion would erupt into general strikes that would bring the mercantile operations of the nation to a halt.

Amid the resulting chaos, Miranda Lee-Weston—the president having crossed her Rubicon—would assume her coveted role of Liberty leading the people, remove the Council of Twelve, and bring down the existing government.

All of this could happen.

CHAPTER 30

▼

The Council of Twelve moved its operations to a series of top-secret locations. In the interest of national security, Kurt Striker's office maintained direct communication with the various ministerial command posts.

"I'm afraid Mrs. Lee-Weston's involvement is far more significant than we originally expected," Striker informed Madam Chairwoman and the others during a conference call.

"The president is planning a coup, probably on or sometime near July 4th, the 25th anniversary of Second Independence Day. We have uncovered a facsimile of a rather comical document called *The Certification of America* that declares the council incompetent to govern by reason of insanity. Apparently, the president plans to use the declaration to stir up dissent among the earthlings. The psychiatrists, as it turns out, were recruited as signatories."

"I trust you have placed Mrs. Lee-Weston under arrest."

"I'm sorry to report that the president has gone undercover."

"When can we expect her apprehension, Commander?"

"Thanks to the authority you have granted my office, my lady, we are accumulating information rapidly. We've recruited several double agents who will soon be able to disclose Mrs. Lee-Weston's whereabouts."

"We will tolerate no mistakes, Commander."

The remark stung, but Striker maintained control. He knew exactly where Miranda Lee-Weston had established her primitive command post, but there was little to gain by interfering with her activities too soon.

"You can trust the Office of Homeland Security explicitly," he said, with as much grace as he was able to muster.

Following his conference with the council, Striker spoke privately with George Salinger.

"Our intelligence has determined that Alfred Dobson is a British secret agent, my lord. We suspect he is an assassin with orders to eliminate you and your family, perhaps as early as your impending return to Haworth Manor."

"I'm also afraid your son Jack has become a signatory to the president's bizarre document."

"Do you expect she may be able to release the damned thing?"

"I'm not overly concerned if she does," Striker said.

"Well I am, Commander Striker! I don't want the Salinger name sullied by this affair."

"We are doing everything possible to contain the situation, my lord. But I wanted to know what you wish me to do with your son."

"Jack has brought enough grief to me and to his family. I want him eliminated, Commander Striker. As soon as possible."

"I see," Striker said. "Are you suggesting direct assassination, or would you like to offer your son…shall we say, a challenge?"

"What do you mean?"

"Well," Striker said. "I could arrange to send him to the streets. It might be interesting to see how your son would fair in a contest of wills with the citizens of his fair city. At the same time, Dr. Salinger may be able to lead us to some of his fellow conspirators."

"Jack has always been an abject coward," the professor said. "If threatened, he will grovel like a beaten dog in the dirt. But if he can be of any use to you, I have no objection to anything you choose to do with him."

"Perhaps you don't know your son, my lord?"

"Make no mistake, Commander Striker, I know Jack very well."

"A small wager might be amusing," Striker suggested.

"I'm not interested in playing games, Commander! But go ahead; send Jack into the city. He won't stand a chance."

"As you wish, my lord."

Kurt Striker deactivated the telecommunication device. He watched the callous face of George Salinger slowly deconstruct. Then, he recalled the holographic image of Jack Salinger. Despite himself, Striker felt a qualm of pity. He considered Dr. Jack Salinger the most unfortunate Angel in America.

CHAPTER 31

▼

The long awaited call, though anticipated, struck Salinger with disturbing finality. The time was shortly before 2:30 P.M. With that call, Salinger realized that he, too, was about to cross his own Rubicon. He was told that the decision to retrieve him by helicopter had been aborted. No reason for the change in plan was given. He was instructed to make his descent to the street and proceed to the newly assigned safe house in his sector.

Salinger unsealed his emergency pack, donned his face and body armor, and checked the Glock, before holstering the weapon. John Mitchell—the sheriff in the village Salinger had visited with the president—had complained about the illegal possession of weapons by renegade earthlings. Scavengers, Mitchell had called such people. Salinger knew he might encounter armed vigilantes anywhere on the street. He activated the GPS unit and checked the coordinates of the safe house. The site was located 5.6 miles from his present position.

Salinger loaded a backpack with food, a few bottles of wine, some chocolate truffles, and a supply of drugs, including a few packs of Mary Js. He suspected a sop or two might be useful. Salinger surveyed his living space for the last time. Then he made his way into the decontamination zone.

He scanned the security monitors and found the space outside clear of intruders. He ran a last minute check with the Centers for Communicable Diseases. The health alert status for his sector was code green.

Jack Salinger took a couple of deep breaths. Then he walked into the corridor outside his living space. He quickly descended the stairwell through the upper 12 floors of the building. He reached the heavily barricaded door that led to the security zone separating Angel quarters from those of the earthlings living on the floors below. The warning signs were very explicit. Angels were advised to proceed further only during emergency situations that threatened loss of life.

Salinger entered his access code into a keypad and then moved into position for the retinal scanning that confirmed his identity as a resident of the building. He declined menu options of sounding an emergency alarm or requesting immediate backup from the security forces assigned to his sector.

The two floors of the security zone that separated Angel and earthling living spaces in Salinger's building had been gutted. The flooring between the two levels had also been removed. He was able to survey the entire space, which was eerily empty except for supporting beams extending from floor to ceiling. A mobile laser probe was slowly scanning the space for intrusion. When Salinger entered the safety zone, the probe immediately locked onto him. He felt strange as the beam of light passed over his face in a strange caress and then peered into his eyes for the mandatory retinal scan. Salinger thought of the earthling, Marveda, whose fatal fight he had watched on television a couple of months earlier.

How had Marveda beaten the system and managed to break into the Angel sector of his building? Maybe he had ascended the outer wall of the structure, bypassing the prohibited zone entirely.

Salinger left the security zone and emerged into the earthling section of the building. He cautiously began to make his descent down one of the darkened stairwells to street level, 34 stories below. He flipped the night vision goggles attached to his helmet into position. His hand went instinctively to the handle of the Glock.

Salinger was three flights from the street when he saw them. Several people were sitting alone in the darkness. They were probably squatters, two adults and two children. The male adult appeared to have heard Salinger. He was peering intently into the darkness.

Salinger activated a magnesium flare. The sudden intense light took the group by surprise. The female and the two children cried out. The woman clasped the two youngsters to her breast. The male rose cautiously to his feet, gripping something, an iron pipe Salinger thought.

"I'm not going to hurt you," Salinger said.

He could now see the male's face clearly. Salinger winced. These people were lepers.

"I'm armed," Salinger said, brandishing the Glock, "but I don't want to harm you. Sit down," he said to the male. "Turn your faces to the wall and don't move. I'm going to pass your position."

The man hesitated a moment, but then took a sitting position next to the others. Salinger slowly moved down the stairwell to the landing and cautiously eased past the group. None of the people could resist staring at him as he passed by. The center of the female's face had been deformed grotesquely by the disease. He could see that both of the children were infected. All of these people would be shot on sight by the security forces or arrested and taken into permanent quarantine. Salinger had heard the rumors. He did not want to think about what permanent quarantine really meant.

The bones of several small animals were scattered about the landing. The group had been living on rats. A makeshift latrine gave off a pungent stench that made Salinger retch as he cautiously moved past the group. Once he had reached the lower staircase, Salinger extracted some food from his pack and placed it on the landing. The male watched Salinger intently and stared at the packet greedily.

"When the light goes out, don't try to follow me," he warned. I can see you in the dark." He pointed to his night vision lenses. Then he cautiously moved on. When he reached the next landing, the flare slowly died out. Jack Salinger was enveloped once again in darkness.

The intense mid-afternoon light on the street was momentarily painful as Salinger emerged from the building. He moved quickly to the center of the street, checked the bearing on the GPS module, and began to move in the direction of the safe house.

The street was deserted. The new American flag flapped irritatingly in the soft breeze. As Salinger proceeded, he tried to pinpoint areas of potential cover in case he encountered a security patrol.

Most of the storefront windows had been broken out. Salinger was able to peer into the lobbies of some of the buildings. An occasional human form could be seen lying against an inside wall. The stench was beyond comprehension. The odor stung Salinger's nostrils. He read gaudily painted graffiti aloud with exaggerated concentration, trying to keep himself anchored to reality.

People were milling about in small groups in the doorways and storefront alcoves. Salinger brandished the Glock from side to side in warning.

"Angel," several people taunted in mocking singsong, "have you come down to play with us?"

Salinger checked the GPS. The virtual map of the city streets was detailed. At the first intersection he turned right. He was relieved to see the distance off slowly diminishing.

Peering into the monitor, Salinger traced the course of the small river mean-dered through the city. A few blocks ahead, he could make out a two-lane bridge, but the structure was heavily barricaded and occupied by a small contingent of security personnel. He was forced to make a diversion along the course of the stream in search of some means of reaching the opposite bank. A few unoccupied makeshift shacks, several stands of trees, and dense shrubbery provided cover.

As Salinger rounded a curve in the course of the stream, he was disappointed to see that the next bridge had been blown. Moored to the bank, however, he spied a small boat. He cautiously moved forward.

When he reached the vicinity of the boat, he stopped to reconnoiter the area. At first he saw no one, but as he cautiously approached the scow he was startled when an old woman ran into the open and began to shout at him.

"You're a long way from Paradise, Angel," she taunted. "You better fly away before you get into trouble."

Salinger made a few threatening gestures with the Glock.

"Don't come any closer," he warned. "I'm going to cross the river in this boat."

"Not on your life," the woman declared. "Take a good look at the water, Angel."

Salinger glanced at the greenish-brown stream, which was rank with raw sew-age and other detritus, including the bobbing corpses of several dead rats.

"You fall in that," the old crone said, "and you won't last a minute."

"Who says I'm going to fall in?" Salinger challenged.

"Me and my lads, Angel. We'll stove in your hull from the bridge if you lay a hand on that boat."

Several young boys made their presence known briefly, before ducking back under cover at the old woman's command.

"This river is as foul as the Styx, Angel. In fact, folks around here call me Charon's grandam. Now, I could ferry you across into hell, which lies just over there on the other side. For a consideration, of course."

"I have some food," Salinger suggested.

The old woman shook her head in refusal.

"I don't need your food, Angel," the woman said, "but I was wondering if you might be carryin' some drugs."

"I can give you some Serenity 400," Salinger said. "Six tablets. Three now, and three more when we get to the other side."

"Deal, Angel."

Salinger handed the three tablets to the woman and then boarded the small skiff, followed by his ragged gondolier, who was struggling to stuff the pills into a sack. The effort caused the vessel to rock precariously. Salinger assumed the woman was in her sixties, but he realized she might be considerably younger. Her face was painted in gaudy splotches of blue and gold. The crazed expression on her face was highlighted by her obvious disdain for him. Salinger peered warily into eyes as cold as those of a coiled snake.

Despite the light breeze coursing down the stream, a sickly miasma wafted into the air as the boat rocked with each thrust of the pole. The old woman's minions were carefully watching the progress of the scow from crouched positions near the gap in the partially blown bridge.

"He'll kill you, Nan" one voice cried out. "As soon as you get him to the other side."

The old woman appeared to pay no attention to the warning. She made steady strokes with the pole until the small vessel reached the opposite bank. Salinger handed her the three additional pills and disembarked.

He then raised the Glock and pointed the weapon at his strange river pilot.

"You wouldn't waste a bullet on a defenseless old earthling, would you, Angel?" the woman asked. "Or maybe you'd rather not make any noise?"

The skiff wobbled slightly as the old woman tried to maintain her composure. Salinger lowered the weapon and turned to walk away.

"Have fun in hell, Angel," his gondolier taunted, as she began her return voyage across the figurative river Styx. "You won't last the day."

CHAPTER 32

▼

Two blocks beyond the river, Salinger reversed direction in order to bring himself back on course to his objective. He made his away along the street keeping as close to the cover of the buildings as possible. Ahead, Salinger could see that his passage opened onto a square. Garbled noise was issuing from a megaphone. He debated finding a place of relative refuge and waiting for nightfall.

As Salinger approached the square, the voice from the megaphone became more distinct. Orders were being given to earthlings milling about in the center of the open space. Salinger entered one of the buildings that bordered the city center. He cautiously made his way up a stairwell to the third floor. He opened the door to the first room he encountered, suspecting the windows inside would overlook the plaza.

The space Salinger stepped into was long and narrow. One or more smaller rooms had obviously been conjoined. About twenty figures—women of various ages, including several children—were kneeling on mats strewn about the floor. The women were intoning an eerily enchanting mantra. The group, with their backs to Salinger, had not heard him enter. The odor of pungent incense pervaded the space.

Sandalwood, or maybe musk, he speculated with odd detachment.

Several of the participants were gathered beneath a young woman who had been bound to a crucifix that was mounted to the far wall. Her head was drooping on her breast and she appeared to have lost consciousness. A vertical strip of skin had been removed from her abdominal wall. Her body had also been pierced in several places, across the forehead, at the nipples of the breasts, and near both wrists and ankles. Blood was streaming from these various wounds. In turn, the celebrants approached the suspended figure and suckled the breasts or drew blood into their mouths from one or more of the other wounds by sucking at the fingertips or toes. Each communicant then consumed a small piece of flesh hewn from the strip that had been removed from the sacrificial victim's body.

As she turned away from her communion of flesh and blood, one of the women spied Salinger. A strange hissing sound emerged from the communicant's bloodstained mouth. Fear riveted Salinger to the floor.

He found himself confronted by a cadre of females whose faces were twisted grotesquely with rage. The gown of one of the women fell open; her body was scarred in locations identical to the fresh wounds of the present victim. Two of the communicants began to slink toward Salinger. He switched the Glock to stun mode and shot both his assailants, bringing the advance of the rest of the group to a halt.

"I don't want to hurt anyone," Salinger said, sweeping the Glock from side to side.

Several of the women were in animated conversation. Salinger couldn't make out everything being said, but it was clear the group was contemplating a collective assault. Doubtless, his body and blood would become the next Eucharist for this strange group of celebrants, should the group have its way with him.

Salinger edged toward the door. Just before he reached the exit, a small girl rushed in his direction wielding a wooden cudgel. She tried to strike him, as she spewed a stream of invective and hatred. He could not bring himself to shoot her, even with the weapon in stunning mode. He grabbed at the stick and wrested it from the child's hand.

"You don't understand, I'm not your enemy," he said, but the young girl's eyes, brimming with tears of anger and scorn, gave no hint of comprehension.

Salinger backed out of the room and closed the door. He waited in the hallway with the Glock at the ready for several moments. When the chanting resumed, he moved further along the hall. The next room he tried was empty and the door contained an old, but serviceable, deadbolt. He debated entrapping himself inside, but the relative security of the location was persuasive. Salinger felt he would be able to rappel to the street should escape become necessary.

From his vantage at the open window, Salinger surveyed the scene in the square using the binocular lenses in his night vision goggles. The late afternoon sun had broken through an opening in the clouds and was illuminating the spires of a Gothic styled church. The building was being used as a food distribution center. Earthlings had apparently been trucked into the square by heavily armed security forces. From a tower, staging instructions were issuing from the megaphone. Various groups disembarked from the vehicles or boarded again after picking up the government dole of bread, beer, and a small supply of vegetables. Some of the earthlings were directed to places in the food lines. Others appeared to be competing for openings at one of the scattered collection points where work assignments were being made.

Salinger scanned the signs set up in front of pavilions administering the various work details. People were wanted for corpse retrieval or disposal, street and road repair, sewer inspection, or food processing activities.

Salinger panned the scene, locking on to the faces of some of the individuals in the crowd. Defiant anger was the prevailing expression.

Suddenly an altercation broke out. Salinger zeroed in on two earthlings who appeared to be arguing over their respective positions in one of the food lines. The men fell to the ground mauling one another. Three members of the security force broke up the melee and dragged the two combatants to an open area a few yards from the line. The men were ordered to their knees and then were summarily shot in the head from behind. The bodies pitched forward to the concrete.

A collective gasp and then an ominous groan rose from the crowd. The contingent of armed Angels brandished weapons at the group until the cries of protest died off. Then the earthlings began to thump their feet on the pavement in unison. The drumming continued for several minutes until the furious Angels began to decimate the crowd. Every tenth individual was dragged from the ranks and shot on the spot. Finally the sound of protest slowly died away, leaving nearly twenty people lying dead on the ground.

Salinger stared blankly into the square. Revulsion and disgust at what he had just witnessed stuck in his throat.

Salinger waited in the building until the sun began to set. The brilliant golden illumination of the church spires in the waning light was incongruously beautiful. The effect contrasted strikingly with the dismal human drama playing out on the square. Finally, the crowd began to break up. Salinger watched the exodus of the various groups until the plaza was empty. Then he left his observation post, cautiously vacated the building, and resumed his advance toward the safe house.

With the onset of twilight, earthlings began to emerge in greater numbers to mill about the streets. An odd collection of individuals in garish costumes fashioned from disparate elements of every kind began to monitor Salinger's progress with interest. He confronted people with strangely painted faces and bodies. The earthlings taunted him mercilessly.

A young woman seductively bared her breasts.

"Wanna go round the world, Angel?" she taunted, pointing in the direction of an overturned vehicle that was doubtless her place of business.

Salinger was sweating profusely. He was still a mile and a half from his objective. He tried to concentrate on his surroundings to diffuse the danger of the situation. He seemed to be running a gauntlet in slow motion. He scanned the streets ahead for security patrols.

Several objects were hurled at him. All of the latent cruelty and basic bestiality of the human animal nauseated Salinger. Images of the many beautiful paintings he had studied of the martyrdom of Stephen by stoning in the streets or the death of Sebastian by bow and arrow scrolled through Salinger's mind.

Salinger reached a building that contained a large interior mall. His instincts urged him to leave the street, at least temporarily. He might be able to reach his objective more safely by working his way through an interior corridor.

Suddenly a bullet struck the pavement just ahead of him and ricocheted in the direction of the group of earthlings following closely behind. The earthlings scattered. Salinger lurched to the side, surprised he had not been hit. He rushed into the lobby of the building. From the shelter of the entryway he carefully surveyed the street. No military patrol was in sight. He saw no one approaching and no one on any of the surrounding rooftops. Salinger could not decide where the shot had come from. He would have to attempt an interior passage to a possible exit in the rear of the building. He gripped the Glock tightly and quickly bolted inside.

Cautiously, Salinger made his way along the corridor. The place had been a shopping mall at one time. Dim light was suffusing into the space from skylights in the ceiling. Mannequins, stripped of their clothing and with gaudily painted faces, stared at Salinger from display alcoves. Store logos and decrepit signs advertising sales promotions were gathering dust. Crude shelters had been set up in several of the abandoned stores. Some of these were occupied.

One group of earthlings was morbidly fascinating. Despite his anxiety about a pursuing assailant, Salinger could not help watching a macabre procedure underway in one of the shelters. A middle-aged man was stretched on the floor. He was naked. Four individuals were holding his arms and legs. The four were intoning a chant of some kind. The man had a stick tightly clenched between his teeth. He was soaking wet with sweat.

An individual whose face was painted in alternating red and black stripes was bending over the man, probing into an incision that had been made in the abdomen. This primitive surgeon looked up at Salinger with a challenging sneer. He had extracted a portion of the man's bowel. Salinger could see at once that the stricken earthling's appendix was abscessed and gangrenous.

An impulse to do something overcame Salinger's sense of danger. He moved toward the group. He had last participated in surgery in medical school.

"I'm a doctor," he said. "Let me help you."

The operator appeared unsure how to respond.

Suddenly, the sick man began to convulse. His body contracted with a spasm. His head was thrown back and his torso lifted from the floor. His four restrainers struggled to hold him down. Then the man's body relaxed onto the floor. He twitched convulsively several times, but then—following a prolonged gasp—he stopped breathing. Before Salinger could reach him he had suffered cardiac arrest and was dead.

The group began to curse Salinger, blaming him for the man's death. His efforts to explain were pointless. The profession he had callously rejected had ruthlessly rejected him. He edged along the corridor, moving further into the bowels of the building.

"Hey, Birdie, wanna come fly with me?" a female voice called out.

Salinger was startled by the unexpected sound. He noticed a young female standing in a seductive slouch in one of the entryways.

"Wanna wrap Momma up in your pretty wings, Angel?"

Salinger glanced toward the door through which he had entered the building. A figure slipped inside and darted into the shadows. Salinger directed the woman into her place of business, pointing with the Glock.

"Keep quiet," he demanded. "I'll use this if I have to."

The woman held up her hands in mock surrender and laughed raucously.

"I told you to shut the fuck up," Salinger said.

She locked her lips ceremoniously with a smirk.

He directed the earthling to the back of the room. He then took a position close to the entrance and waited.

Salinger suspected his pursuer was an armed scavenger, a body stripper like one of those John Mitchell, the magistrate from the village Salinger had visited with Mrs. Lee-Weston, had described.

Salinger watched the figure cautiously pick its way from one area of relative cover to the next. Salinger switched the Glock to stunning mode, waited until his target was in view, and then downed his pursuer with a single shot. The scavenger had probably not anticipated an armed adversary.

What took place next shocked Jack Salinger. He was overcome by intense unmitigated rage. He walked over to his downed adversary, flipped the switch on the Glock to lethal mode, and pointed the weapon at the back of the man's head. Just as he was about to pull the trigger, Salinger visualized a sudden unmistakable image of his father's face. His hand trembling, he slowly lowered the weapon to his side.

A sudden high-pitched cry came from behind Salinger. The young woman bolted from her sanctuary, dropped to the ground, and began to strip the clothing from the scavenger. Like a shark in feeding frenzy, she took everything useful from the body, leaving the man lying naked on the floor. The girl was very careful to avoid any contact with the unconscious man's blood, which was oozing from a small laceration on his forehead. Salinger noticed the telltale lesions of Kaposi's sarcoma on the man's skin. He was in the advanced stages of HIV infection.

The girl gathered her spoils, including the scavenger's weapon, and ran back into her asylum. At the doorway, she turned and leveled the gun at Salinger.

"I'm wearing body armor and you're not," Salinger said. "You better think twice about a shootout, sweetheart."

The girl lowered the firearm and moved inside. Salinger followed her.

Salinger eased past the dust-covered shelves and empty clothing racks. The eerie faces of several naked manikins leered at him seductively.

At the rear of the former apparel shop, the girl opened the door to a concealed passageway. She urged Salinger to follow her inside.

"There may be more of them," she prudently suggested.

They made their way down a cramped corridor, through another concealed entryway, and finally entered a room that appeared to be the young woman's living space.

She motioned toward a garishly upholstered settee, an old turn of the 21st century antique, its fabric sewn over with an array of patches. Salinger, after surveying the area but finding no evidence of additional occupants, finally settled into the ancient couch. The muscles of his back and neck were knotted with tension.

He studied his hostess's face for the first time. He saw that she was actually quite young, probably no older than fifteen or so. She was extremely attractive and nubile. He searched her face for telltale signs of infection.

"Well, Birdie," she said mockingly, "you seem to have come a long way from your little heaven up on high. What brings you down to earth?"

"Actually, I'm a fugitive," he admitted.

They sat confronting one another. They were two people from totally diverse worlds. Two fellow Americans, he thought sarcastically.

"What's your name?" he asked.

"Leah,' she said. "What's yours?"

"Jack," he said. "Jack Salinger."

"So what have you got for Momma, Jack Salinger, hidden under those pretty wings of yours?"

Salinger unpacked some food and opened one of the bottles of wine. He took out a Mary J, lit it, and passed it to his young hostess.

"I can't share this with you," he said. "So I'm going to light one of my own."

"I'm not sick,' she said indignantly.

"Women of your profession usually say that," he scoffed, taking a long welcome hit on his own joint.

"Hey, you've got that wrong, Angel!" she said with disdain. "I don't do street sex. My momma did that and she died when I was eleven."

"Seems to me you invited me to come what...come fly with you...to use your earlier expression."

"That was only to get you into my clutches, Jack the Angel. I never intended to fuck you, Birdie. I'm just a professional hustler."

"So I guess I'm really safe being here with you now," Salinger suggested.

"Hey, I've scored bigger with you, Birdie, than I have in months. Fair is fair. You're safe with me."

"Are you sure you're safe with me?" he chided.

"I'm not sure about that at all," she said, with an impish grin.

"I should leave," Salinger said, gathering his gear.

"Where are you headed?" Leah asked.

Salinger showed the girl the GPS image of the surrounding territory and pointed out his objective.

"I know where that place is, but I would advise you to wait until dark before moving out."

"I thought cities were supposed to be safer by day?" he suggested.

"Not this city," Leah said. "Besides, I can take you there. I know some passageways on the inside. Between the security patrols and the night people, you'd never make it through the open streets on your own."

Salinger relaxed into his seat on the couch.

"Well, I guess you're stuck with me for a while," he said.

"I've had worse company, Birdie."

Salinger rummaged in his pack, extracted a chocolate truffle, and passed it to Leah.

"What is it?" she asked.

"Chocolate. I suspect you haven't had much of that before. Try it; you'll like it."

Leah was overcome by a bout of cannabis induced giggling, as she examined the gold foil wrapper.

"I've heard of this stuff," she said. "It's not poison, is it?"

"Well no, but chocolate can be addicting."

Leah tried some. One taste and she settled into a noisy, but very sensual consumption of the tiny delicacy.

"Got any more of this stuff, Birdie?"

Salinger passed her a second truffle.

Leah became voluble. Salinger was fascinated. She was just a kid, really. He wondered how she had managed to survive. She had as many questions about his life as he did about hers. The hour of remaining daylight passed quickly.

CHAPTER 33

▼

Leah was a street-smart kid; she was tough and ruthless in ways that should not have been necessary. She insisted that she would always live alone.

"Other people complicate things too much," she explained.

She joined work details whenever possible, including occasional corpse retrieval following the epidemics.

"I hate to pick up the children though," she said.

Jack could not help express interest in how she managed to stay out of trouble.

"You have to watch your back," Leah explained. "My mother taught me a lot before she died. Nobody messes with me anymore. How about another one of the those chocolates, Birdie?"

Salinger passed her another truffle. He concluded Leah was very lucky, despite her professed possession of street smarts.

"I don't do sex either, like I told you. That always gets you into trouble. I'm a big girl and I've learned how to take care of myself, if you know what I mean, Birdie.

"Actually, I don't like it much, sex I mean," Leah added. "When I was a little younger, a scavenger broke in here one night and tried something. But I got him by slipping a downer into his beer. Then I tied him up and cut off his thing and both of his nuts."

Leah giggled raucously, as she wiped dripping chocolate from her chin.

"You shoulda heard him scream, Birdie. I had to gag him to shut him up."

"What happened to him?" Salinger asked.

"I let him bleed to death," Leah said nonchalantly. "Then I got rid of him. I'm not sure, but I think the lepers got him. Serves him right for ruining my bed."

Salinger described his experience earlier that afternoon with the strange congregation of female communicants.

"Are you familiar with that group?" he asked.

"Yeah, those are the Sisters of Eve," Leah said. "They tried to recruit me a couple of times, but I'm not into that weird religious stuff."

"I assume they don't think much of men."

"You got that right, Birdie. You're lucky you got out of there alive."

"I suspect I might have ended up on the cross," he suggested.

"No way, Birdie. They don't use men in their ceremonies. They would have killed you for sperm. They know a lot about getting babies without having sex."

"They use artificial insemination?"

"Yeah. If they can find some male who isn't infected, they milk his sperm and then conduct this very weird fertilization ritual. The women all have sex with the mother to be and then they inject the guy's sperm with a syringe at the end of the ceremony. After one or two of the Sisters get pregnant, they sacrifice the sperm donor to Eve as retribution for the false accusations made against the first human female by the old religions. The Sisters of Eve call the aftermath of the fertilization ceremony, and the killing of the donor, virgin birth with atonement."

Salinger shuddered. The fluid he thought he had been in danger of losing to the so-called Sisters of Eve had not been blood after all.

"The government provides you with some food," Salinger suggested, changing the subject. "How does that work?"

"They come for us in trucks once a week for each district," Leah explained. "You have to listen for the loudspeakers and the announcement of the number assigned to your section. They drive you to the square and you line up for a dole of bread and beer. There are vegetables, if you're lucky.

"In the old days, farmers would bring in produce and set up a market once a week. But the scavengers starting picking them off on the way into the city. Now, the government brings in vegetables and occasionally fruit under armed guard. When you get to the square, you can also sign up for one of the work details. The units come in handy getting things from the black market."

"Things like what?" Salinger asked.

"Drugs, mostly. Like vitamins, or what they call antibiotics. You can get extra food, too, sometimes."

"Some people eat rats?"

"The lepers do. That's often all they can get. They eat rats and corpses, like I said. Some of the others eat rats too, but not me, Birdie! That's where I draw the line. I don't eat rats."

"So what do you do for entertainment?" Salinger asked.

"Entertainment!" Leah scoffed. "I try to stay alive for entertainment. I could watch the televised stuff, like the executions and the fights, but the assembly centers are very creepy places. Girls without mates never go there, if they're smart. I assume you realize, Birdie, that I'm very smart."

"What about books?"

"I'm not big on reading," Leah admitted. "I mean I can read, don't get me wrong. You can get books from the black market hustlers. But mostly, I just like to sing the old songs my mother taught me, if I ever have any leisure time, which is not very often."

Later that evening, Leah described the system used in the earthling territories for distribution of information, real information that complemented the censored releases on the state supported news network.

"Earthlings on the large estates have been our best source," she explained. "Most of them know how to use the computers in the manor houses. They take big risks using the machines at night, but over the years they've been able to intercept communications not meant for earthlings.

"We've developed a network of circulators who carry the real news from place to place, something like an old system they used to call the pony express hundreds of years ago. But I doubt you've ever heard of such a thing, Birdie.

"The couriers carry messages, too, sort of like the old postal system. We don't have electronic mail like you Angels have. Some of the earthlings in the military ask the carriers to deliver units to their families for them, but that takes a lot of trust. Most of the troops wait until they can get leave, but that doesn't happen very frequently.

"Most of these couriers memorize important information and give reports to local news agents, who pass the word in the assembly halls or on the streets. Miranda has been using the system for years to keep us posted about the coming war."

"Miranda?"

"She's our leader, our soul sister, Birdie, even though you Angels call her your president. You should see her. She's the most beautiful woman in America. Most of the people I know would follow her anywhere, when the time comes."

"Do you think the time is near?" he asked.

"Oh yeah, Birdie, a big war is coming. Some people say the battle of Armageddon will be fought soon. An important sign that the revolution is about to begin is supposed to appear any day now. I can't wait to see what Miranda will do."

As the evening progressed, perhaps under the influence of the marijuana, the wine or even the truffles, Leah became amorous. She began to flirt with Salinger.

"You know, Birdie, I could change my mind about having sex with you," she said. "Like I said, I'm not sick."

"You're a very beautiful young woman, Leah," Salinger said. "I know being with you would be wonderful," he admitted, with a twinge of honest regret. "But I'm in love with someone else. I can't bring myself to be unfaithful."

"You must love her very much."

"More than anything in the world," Salinger said with candor. "I hope when you finally decide to give yourself to someone, Leah, you will wait for someone who will love you as much as I love my friend."

"Is she your life mate?"

"No, not yet," Salinger said. "She's not in my economic class. We can't be together."

"I'm not in your economic class either, I guess," Leah said.

"No, I guess you're not, but many of us are trying to change that."

"So you are involved, Birdie," Leah said. "In the revolution, I mean."

"Yes," Salinger admitted. "I'm very much involved."

CHAPTER 34

▼

Salinger's chronometer fascinated Leah. A little after 11 P.M, the girl led him through a labyrinth of corridors and passageways in the direction of the safe house. Some sections of the trek passed through alleys and parts of the street. A full moon, glowing dimly through a mantle of mid-level clouds, added sufficient illumination to navigate without the use of Salinger's night vision gear.

Fires, surrounded by groups of shadowy figures, were burning outside a number of the buildings. Salinger was struck most by the realization that these people had almost nothing to do. Occasional shadowy figures—one of them a group of flagellants, Leah explained—could be seen moving through the mist, but the pair made steady progress until they reached a narrow passageway between two large buildings.

"I don't like this," Salinger said.

"I don't either," Leah agreed. "But I don't see anything, do you?"

Salinger surveyed the location with his night vision apparatus, but no one was visible.

Cautiously, the two moved into the constricted passage. They had reached the midpoint, when four male earthlings suddenly leapt from second floor windows, landing in the alleyway in front of and behind Salinger and the girl. Before Salinger was able to respond, one of the men had grabbed Leah and was holding a knife to her throat.

"Well, look what we have here," he said. "Fresh meat and an Angel. This is our lucky day, lads."

The group, all four armed with knives, laughed raucously.

"Show us her tits," one of the men demanded.

The man holding Leah began to fumble with her shirt. Salinger had been sweeping the group with the Glock, warning the parrying men off. He pointed the weapon at the man holding Leah.

"I'm going to blow your fucking head off," he threatened.

Leah's assailant stopped trying to expose the girl's breasts. He began to use her body as cover.

"You better be the best shot on earth, Angel, or your little friend here is going to take the first hit. And if you blow away one of my boys, I'm going to slit her throat from ear to ear."

"You can't get us all, Angel," another one of the assailants jeered. "Those of us you don't get are going to take your skin off, just like you bastards do to us on television."

Salinger was seething with rage. Without warning, he switched the Glock to stunning mode and shot Leah. As the girl's body suddenly slumped, he switched the firearm back to lethal mode and shot her adversary in the face. Then he lurched to the side, taking out the other man standing in front of him. The other two men stabbed at him from behind, but missed. Salinger whirled and shot them both at point blank range.

Leah was down, but she had not been cut.

Salinger walked methodically to each of the four men. Two were dead, including the apparent ringleader. Two were alive, but badly wounded.

"Don't kill me, Angel," one of them pleaded.

Without a word, Salinger shot both of the men in the face.

He sat down, holding Leah in his arms until she revived. As he waited for her to regain consciousness, Salinger wrestled with the fact that he had just killed four human beings in cold blood. He wanted to feel remorse of some kind. What he did sense was exhilaration. What had Mrs. Lee-Weston said? People revert to bestiality if the restraints of civilization are taken from them? Again, the president had been at least partially correct. Beasts kill from necessity. Jack Salinger realized he had immensely enjoyed taking four human lives.

Salinger looked at the sky. A dark bird was flying overhead, a hawk or a crow perhaps. Salinger thought about his brother Martin and the savage art of falconry.

"You've been wrong about me, Father," Salinger said aloud. "You've been wrong about me all of my life. I'm a Salinger, Father, a Salinger just like you."

CHAPTER 35

▼

Leah was groggy until she noticed the bodies of the four assailants.

"That was the closest call I've ever had!" she said. "I really thought they had us. They were smart, coming for us out of the windows that way. But you really outfoxed them, Birdie! Shooting me like that was brilliant."

Leah reached up and kissed him on the cheek. Then she embraced him. He could sense, however, that she was trembling.

"I guess I owe you my life, Birdie," she said.

The great human warmth Jack Salinger should have been feeling was crowded out by lingering, unmitigated rage.

Shortly after midnight, Leah and Salinger reached the safe house, which was located in the basement of an abandoned bookstore.

Salinger presented his identification module. His retinal scans confirmed his identity. Leah's scans did not trip a security alarm. He and his companion were admitted and led to the headquarters of the squadron commander.

Salinger and Leah entered the room. The commander reviewed the identification data. Abruptly, he rose from his seat and called his squadron of four men and two women to attention.

"This is Dr. Jack Salinger," the commander said with enthusiasm.

The six members of the squadron snapped to attention and saluted sharply.

"Welcome, Sir," they called out in unison.

Salinger was taken aback by the enthusiastic greeting. Leah, too, was surprised.

"I guess you *are* involved, Birdie," she said.

The commander retrieved a small card from his desk.

"We received an advance copy a few days ago," he explained. He handed the card to Salinger. The facsimile of *The Certification of America* displayed Salinger's signature, clearly visible just below Miranda Lee-Weston's.

Leah eagerly examined the document and then slowly parsed out Salinger's name.

"I can't read it all," she said, "but it looks impressive, Birdie."

The squadron personnel came up to shake Salinger's hand and offer thanks and congratulations. Salinger was embarrassed by the sudden celebrity, but moved by the emotion on the faces of the president's troops.

"We want you to know how much we appreciate the tremendous sacrifice you have made for us," one of the recruits said warmly, her voice choking noticeably as she spoke.

"We have orders to relocate immediately in the event of any contact, Dr. Salinger," the commander explained. "You and your escort will leave for the president's command post within the hour. The rest of us will move to our next assigned location in the morning."

"When did the president inform you that I would be coming here?" Salinger asked.

"What do you mean?" the commander countered.

Salinger explained the change in plans the day before, from air evacuation to movement over the ground to the safe house.

"We had no specific indication that you *would* arrive here," the commander said. "Our last orders from the president's command post arrived over a week ago. We received your identification data, but we were given no specific time of arrival. In fact, our impression was that you would be moved to the president's location by air."

Salinger looked into the commander's face. He tried not to betray his sudden confusion.

Later, Salinger spoke to the squadron leader about Leah.

"We can use all of the warm bodies we can get," he said. "If she's willing to serve, we can find an assignment for her."

Leah had monitored the exchange with interest.

"So, Birdie, you want me to have a regular job for a change?" she suggested.

"If that's what you want," he said.

"I don't suppose I can go with you?" she said.

"No, Leah, I'm afraid that's not possible."

"So this is goodbye then, is it Birdie?"

Salinger put his arms around Leah and drew her to him.

"I'll miss you," he said.

She tried to avoid looking into his face, but he could see the tears in her eyes.

"Hey, think about me," she managed with bravado, "I don't get to meet a famous patriot every day."

Salinger extracted one of several spare flashcards containing his holographic image from his jacket pocket. He handed the memory card to Leah.

"Keep this," he said. "Someday you will have access to a modern computer and you will have learned how to use one. This card contains my holograph. By accessing the image, you'll have something to remember me by."

"I guess you think I'm never going to see you again."

"I don't know what might happen in the days ahead," Salinger said.

The girl clutched the small object to her breast. Salinger could see she was trying to suppress her emotions.

"Make the country a better place, Leah," Salinger said, before he turned and slowly walked away.

CHAPTER 36

▼

Upon arrival at the president's command post, Salinger was immediately led into Mrs. Lee-Weston's field office.

"Why weren't you at the heliport when the aircraft arrived to pick you up, Dr. Salinger?" the president asked. Mrs. Lee-Weston's voice was sharp, her anger uncharacteristic.

Salinger became defensive as he explained the countermanding order and the instructions he was given to proceed to the ground level safe house.

President Lee-Weston immediately summoned her second in command.

"General Ryan," she said, "I'm afraid our security has been breached. I want you to relocate our headquarters immediately.

"Come with me," Mrs. Lee-Weston said to Salinger. "There is someone here I want you to meet."

Salinger followed the president into a conference room. A soldier in field fatigues was peering at the graphics displayed by a large computer module; the man was intently examining a topographical map suspended in space. As the door opened, he turned in the president's direction.

"Adam?" Salinger managed. "Adam Kennedy?"

Salinger had not seen his old roommate in eight years. Adam Kennedy was partially bald, prematurely gray, and was wearing a full beard. He resembled an over-sized leprechaun. His eyes, however, had not changed. He still had the old fire.

"Well, Jack, I can't say I'm all that glad to see you," Kennedy said. "I wasn't happy when the president told me you were going to be one of the signatories."

Salinger stood with his left elbow resting on his clenched right fist, the fingers of his left hand compressing the skin below his mouth. His eyes were fixed on Kennedy's.

"I took advantage of my position, but I never sold you out, Adam," he said.

"I'd like to believe that, Jack."

"Believe it," Salinger said.

Adam Kennedy said nothing immediately. He stood watching Salinger's face intently. President Lee-Weston was carefully monitoring the exchange. Adam Kennedy looked from Salinger to the president, who quietly nodded.

"Well, I guess we have some catching up to do," he said, finally grasping Salinger's hand.

The reunion between Salinger and his old friend proceeded haltingly at first, but recollection of their youthful collaboration, and Jack's sincere interest in the harrowing tale of Kennedy's narrow escape gradually wore down any lingering animosities Adam harbored. A glass or two of Irish whiskey accelerated the thaw.

Adam Kennedy had been field commander for a guerilla unit in support of the president since the assassination of her husband; he had been instrumental in organizing grass roots support for Miranda Lee-Weston's insurrection. He had more than a few war stories to tell his old friend.

"I think you could serve best as a non-combatant in one of our field hospitals, Dr. Salinger," the president suggested, when the subject turned to Salinger's future assignment. "I suspect you have some skills that could benefit our troops."

"Madam President," Salinger said, "I've never had any real interest in medicine. That has been my greatest failing...as a physician. I want to be assigned to a field unit," he said. "I would like to begin training immediately. I'd like to serve under Adam's command...if he will have me. I have a lot to prove to Commander Kennedy."

The president was pleased when Adam Kennedy nodded in affirmation.

In the days ahead, Jack Salinger received intensive training—a crash course— in the nuances of guerilla warfare.

CHAPTER 37

▼

With release of *The Certification of America*, all 56 signatories were declared collaborators disloyal to the government of the United States of America. They were tried in absentia and sentenced to death. Similarly, Miranda Lee-Weston was declared an enemy of the state. Anyone providing information that led to her capture, or the capture of any of the signatories, was to be awarded the nation's highest civilian citation, membership in the Legion of Sacred Honor.

Disturbing reports of the arrests of several of the signatories reached the command post.

For six agonizing days following the release of the certification, nothing of significance happened. But then work stoppages and sit-down strikes began. Earthlings suffered terrible reprisals. But the protests continued. Transportation slowed, the production of the larger factories fell off drastically, and earthlings all over America threw down their tools and refused to work.

Despite orders to burn all facsimiles upon discovery, the president's *Certification of America* proliferated. Quotations from the document were displayed on placards and were carried through the streets by protesting earthlings. The document was read by increasing numbers of earthlings and Angels. As *The Certification of America* became more widely known, labor unrest spread to the level of general strikes. The military was ordered to begin punishment of the labor force by decimation. Every tenth protesting worker was shot on the spot.

But then, earthlings in the military forces began to refuse to carry out the executions. Initially, some of the Angels from the officer class retaliated by shooting their own insubordinate troops. In response, desertions to the president's army of rebellion began to rise drastically, swelling the ranks of the rebel forces. These crucial personnel brought with them badly needed arms and equipment.

The fragging of hard-line Angel officers also started happening. The executions of protesting earthlings stopped abruptly. A paralyzing standoff developed between Angels loyal to the Council of Twelve and those now devoted to the President of the United States.

Miranda Lee-Weston, now commander-in-chief of a growing army of rebellion, realized that a dramatic gesture was needed to sustain the momentum of the growing civil unrest sweeping the nation. Reluctantly, the President of the United States—with full executive power for the first time since her inauguration—gave a direct, but distasteful order.

CHAPTER 38

▼

Adam Kennedy had been instrumental in orchestrating the escalating surface-to-air missile attacks against Angel aircraft, like the one directed to the helicopter used by Jack Salinger's security force several months earlier.

Kennedy had been increasingly frustrated by the failures of these strikes and the immense cost of the retaliatory measures taken by the government. He was now ready to play his trump card, thanks to the assistance of a group of British undercover agents. One of these had been Commander Alfred Dobson. Dobson had managed—at enormous risk—to bring the final crucial components of an advanced Stinger guidance system into the country.

Field Commander Adam Kennedy had overseen the laborious construction of a small cache of precision Stinger surface-to-air missiles within the borders of the United States. The final guidance components had made the weapons fully operational.

Three ministers of the Council of Twelve had been identified as most vulnerable, based upon a two-year long intelligence operation.

Three of the Stinger missiles had been placed in concealed sites along air routes frequented by the targeted ministers. The element of surprise—and the conceit of the council that such state-of-the-art ordnance would never fall into the hands of the rebels—was the key to the success of the operation.

Jack Salinger had been assigned to one of the three missile batteries.

The National News Service saturated every media outlet in the country with a series of banner headlines, not unlike those used in newspaper accounts during the 19th century.

"COWARDLY TERRORIST ATTACKS AGAINST COUNCIL OF TWELVE"

"Director of Homeland Security calls missile strikes intolerable. Vows swift retaliation."

"FOREIGN INFLUENCE SUSPECTED"

"Nation in mourning. Flags at half-staff. Three ministers believed lost."

"CHEERING EARTHLINGS TAKE TO STREETS. SECURITY FORCES ON FULL ALERT."

"Commander Kurt Striker to address nation."

Information was coming in rapidly, although some of the details were sketchy. The three strikes had occurred in sequence approximately 20 minutes apart. Turbo-choppers bearing three of the ministers had been blown from the sky.

Cardinal Andrew McCarthy, a prelate of the National High Church of Plutus, had been struck as his aircraft was lifting off the heliport of his episcopal mansion. His entourage of eight, including a high-ranking archbishop, had all been lost.

The second chopper had been shot down while passing over one of America's bombed out inner cities. The aircraft was believed to be carrying Dr Marcus Quinlan, president of the Virtual University of Miami. His life mate and three young children were feared aboard. The aircraft had struck an abandoned building and had been completely destroyed. Attempted recovery of identifiable human remains was ongoing.

The third targeted minister, the Honorable Martha Mathison, had gone down in a remote forested area. The minister had survived impact. She had been air evacuated from the crash scene and had undergone in flight surgery. Severe head injuries threatened her survival.

Prior to his address to the nation on the National News Service, Kurt Striker had been summoned to an emergency conference call with the surviving members of the Council of Twelve. Striker surveyed in turn the holographic images suspended in the virtual space of his teleconference module. The ministers were furious. But there was something more in those haggard faces. There was also fear.

"The first breach in national security in twenty-five years has occurred under your watch, Commander Striker. Tell us why we should allow you to remain in office?"

Striker went on the offensive immediately.

"I have warned you repeatedly, my lords and my ladies, that you have hamstrung the Office of Homeland Security. I have pleaded with you to grant access to my department of every weapon in our national arsenal. You have repeatedly refused my requests.

"I take no responsibility for today's events. You will have my resignation within the hour."

"We need not be so hasty, Commander Striker," Madam Chairwoman said.

Striker stared into the video monitor with icy concentration, ticking off the seconds until he was certain the ministers had become sufficiently discomfited. Finally, he bowed toward the faces peering intently at him. Striker concealed his relief behind a cold, impassive mask.

"How could the terrorists have breached our sealed borders and brought these weapons into the country?" George Salinger asked.

"I believe the missiles used were manufactured here in the United States," Striker suggested. "Again, my lord, you were the most vocal advocate of the relaxation of security measures at our borders. Plans for the construction of advanced missiles, or even small but vital components of such weapons, could have bypassed our seriously compromised security checkpoints."

Striker glared at the holographic image of the increasingly uncomfortable George Salinger. "You must advise the council to authorize all measures necessary to fully restore our national defense. I demand a declaration of martial law, the suspension of habeas corpus, and I want the borders of this nation sealed," Striker insisted.

Striker hesitated momentarily, his penetrating eyes sweeping the faces of ministers.

"And I want access codes to our nuclear arsenal and to all biochemical and biological weapons at our disposal. I believe today's events represented only the first phase of Miranda Lee-Weston's attempted coup against your government. I believe, my lords and my ladies, that all of your lives are in grave danger."

"This woman and her co-conspirators have been at large for 15 days, Commander Striker," the ranking member of the council pointed out. "When can we expect her arrest and incarceration?"

Kurt Striker was deferential, but he pointed out the extreme difficulty of pinpointing the location of a mobile adversary with unlimited allies among the common people. He quoted historical instances where key terrorist operatives had never been apprehended during the reign of terror conducted by fundamentalists during the early decades of the 21st century.

"I believe the apprehension of the president and the suppression of the uprising could be expedited if I were given the additional authority I have requested. I must be permitted to direct an appropriate response without constraint," Striker calmly suggested. "I am convinced further attacks against the council are in fact imminent," he added.

The Council of Twelve deliberated for less than an hour. By a vote of seven to two, the remaining ministers approved all of Kurt Striker's demands.

Martial law was authorized and habeas corpus was suspended. Refusal to obey a military order was made punishable by death on the spot, without benefit of trial. All existing constraints against encroachment on personal privacy were removed. The intelligence service was authorized to monitor computer transmissions without cause and to arrest and detain anyone for any purpose at any time.

Kurt Striker was placed in control of the nuclear arsenals of all branches of the American military machine. Most importantly, Striker was given access to several newly developed top secret biological and biochemical weapons. One of these agents—Bionex V-9—was capable of suppressing free will, without causing paralysis or permanent neurological injury.

As Striker prepared to address the nation, the council's rebuff at the beginning of the conference still rankled.

Why had the first act of domestic terrorism in almost twenty-five years happened on his watch? A ludicrous question, Striker thought. It happened, of course, because Kurt Striker permitted it to take place.

The National News Service broadcast a brief statement from the Director of Homeland Security.

"We believe that the former President of the United States—Miranda Lee-Weston—is behind this heinous act of aggression and terrorism. She will be hunted down, captured, and brought to justice swiftly. None of her co-conspirators will go unpunished," Striker began.

"With the concurrence of the surviving members of the Council of Twelve, I have declared that martial law is in effect immediately. Earthlings not under protective escort by security forces will be shot on sight.

"As of this moment, there is no evidence of foreign involvement in the present attacks against us. Should such evidence materialize, we will take swift and appropriate retaliatory action."

Commander Striker said nothing further. The television cameras began to rotate coverage of the three crash sites, interviewing the usual bland series of eyewitnesses who had little to say that had not been carefully scripted beforehand.

A brief statement by President Lee-Weston was illegally broadcast at 3:00 P.M. EST. The president's demeanor was one of compassionate concern. Her face betrayed no evidence of duplicity.

"Our hearts go out to the families of those who have been lost," Mrs. Lee-Weston began. "Acts of social injustice, acts of violence, always take a grave toll on innocent victims.

"We ask all Americans of any economic class to join our effort to reestablish democracy in this great land. We cannot live under a mantle of fear. We cannot labor beneath the weight of oppression.

"We must take this opportunity to reform our government. We must return to the core values that once made America a great and compassionate nation. Correction of the root causes of social disorder are always more humane than retaliation, revenge, and oppression. My fellow Americans, I am calling you to arms, in the name of freedom."

By late afternoon, the National News Service reluctantly reported that all three of the targeted ministers had been killed. Tragically, Dr. Quinlan's immediate family had perished with him.

Before Kurt Striker's declaration of martial law, earthlings in astounding numbers had taken to the streets in celebration of the assassinations. The network broadcast several ruthless attacks on the demonstrators by military security forces in full riot gear. By evening, the death toll among participating earthlings had reached several thousand.

The highly selective National News Network broadcasts did not tell the entire story, however. In fact, increasing numbers of Angels in the military refused to fire on the demonstrators. Angels began to join with earthlings in disarming their superior officers. What appeared to be a brutal suppression of the demonstrating earthlings, as broadcast on national television, became—in many places in America—a standoff in the streets.

CHAPTER 39

▼

The guerilla forces under the command of Adam Kennedy dispersed following the successful attacks. Salinger and the others went under cover and awaited further orders from the president.

Miranda Lee-Weston continued to change the location of her command post daily. The 25th Anniversary of Second Independence Day was rapidly approaching.

In the early afternoon of June 21st the president was sitting alone at her computer module in an isolated underground bunker.

Miranda Lee-Weston's thoughts were racing through history. Which holder of the office had said that the American presidency was the loneliest job in the world? Lincoln once said he was more tired than anyone in the nation.

The president read the Saint Crispin Day speech Henry V had delivered before Agincourt. Then she read Elizabeth's words, delivered near the coast of Dover as the British Navy prepared to engage the Armada. She pulled them all up in sequence, the inspiring orations of Churchill, Roosevelt, and John F. Kennedy. Lastly, she read once again the moving words of President Andrea Rellinger, delivered 26 years ago amid the smoldering ruins of Washington, D.C.

Miranda Lee-Weston opened her file of personal holographs. She sat staring at her husband's image suspended so closely in space, and yet so very far away. She reached out with hesitating fingers, but then slowly withdrew her hand. The pain of that terrible loss had never abated.

If only, she thought.

"Well Weston," she said softly, "has it finally come to this?"

Miranda Lee-Weston choked back the emotion that suddenly constricted her throat. Her shoulders began to shake spasmodically and she was unable to push down a series of sobs. She grasped the edge of the table with both hands, fearing someone might enter the room, until her knuckles blanched white. Slowly, the emotion subsided and she regained control.

"How could they have taken you from me, Weston?" she cried to that lost adored face. "I can't go through this alone."

Reluctantly, the president closed Harold Weston's holograph and brought another image into virtual space. Even without the animation of actual life, this second face was boldly masculine and not at all unattractive.

And yet, this man had callously murdered her husband.

"So, Striker, our little game has entered its final stage," Miranda Lee-Weston said to the image of her enemy and perhaps—in the end—her nemesis. "Are you as sick of all this as I am? I suspect...not."

Mrs. Lee-Weston swept every inch of Kurt Striker's face, searching for some vital point of vulnerability, some soft place to plunge her unrelenting pain.

"I hope I have not underestimated you, Striker," she managed finally. "I expect to defeat you. I will give my life in the attempt. But if that doesn't happen, I want you to bring me rest."

Later that evening—the eve of the summer solstice—President Lee-Weston gathered her officer corps—her most loyal followers—and addressed them. The speech she gave was extemporaneous. Mrs. Lee-Weston used no notes. Many in the audience attempted to transcribe the president's words as they recalled them, but the actual text of her oration was never recorded.

The President of the United States, Commander-in-chief of the new American Revolutionary Army, was able to bring those in her audience to their feet. Those who were present compared the speech to some of the greatest battle orations in history.

The president assured her corps of commanders that, as grandmothers and grandfathers, all of them would proudly tell their grandchildren that they had joined the renewed fight for American freedom on the 25th anniversary of Second Independence Day. She humbly confessed her great sense of inadequacy for the coming battle and placed her trust and the welfare of the nation in the hands of her dedicated followers.

She called the coming national holiday a day of infamy, a callous celebration of the loss of freedom for the majority of Americans. She vowed to fight on to the death—in the streets of the cities and in the villages of a wounded nation—to restore the principles of democracy in the United States of America. She apologized for the great personal sacrifices she was asking her followers to make.

Miranda Lee-Weston also briefly outlined her battle plan. Two hours before dawn, 72 hours prior to the national holiday, the assassinations of the remaining members of the Council of Twelve would take place. The full-scale war of liberation would begin on July 4th, the 25th anniversary of Second Independence Day—the plutocracy's hallowed celebration of the victory of self-interest and greed over the common interests of the American people.

Skulking among the cheering crowd of loyalists were two counterintelligence agents, operatives of the Department of Homeland Security.

CHAPTER 40

▼

Following the successful attacks against the ministers, the three guerilla units had moved to a series of prearranged safe houses. Jack Salinger had become a permanent member of the unit commanded by Adam Kennedy.

Kennedy was briefing the squad on the locations of the next few staging areas. The group would move out at nightfall.

As Kennedy was talking, Salinger sat studying one of the group's GPS units.

"I need to make a diversion, Adam," he said, when the group leader had finished speaking. "I'll be able to triangulate with the rendezvous point at Marsh Creek and rejoin you there."

Kennedy took the GPS from Salinger. He peered at the three-dimensional display of the surrounding terrain and the range and bearing coordinates Salinger had entered.

"I can let you use one of the Hovercraft," Kennedy said. "But you will have to meet us exactly on schedule, Jack," he added. "Otherwise, you'll never find us. By the way, what's so important?"

Adam Kennedy was struck by the expression on Salinger's face.

"I have some unfinished business to attend to at Haworth Manor," Salinger said.

Salinger reached the vicinity of the family estate just after nightfall. He was wearing full combat counter-detection gear. He located the entrance to the concealed tunnel that led underground below the exterior walls into the basement of the manor house. He anxiously punched in the security codes and submitted to retinal scans. His father or Martin might have reprogrammed the device.

Although he was prepared to force entry, Salinger was relieved when he was granted access to the compound.

A small room led from the tunnel near the entrance. Salinger had last been here during the escape drill he and Marla had made during her orientation to Haworth Manor. Salinger collapsed into one of the bunks. He set an alarm for midnight.

When Salinger awoke, he racked the firing mechanism of his Glock. He had extra clips stuffed in his jacket pocket. He was sweating with anticipation, as he moved to the door and began to edge along the tunnel leading to the main house.

Salinger reached the end of the passageway and entered the concealed staircase that led from the tunnel to the family suites on the third floor of the mansion. He checked his firearm and began the ascent.

At the top of the staircase, Salinger stopped to catch his breath. He quietly emerged into the hallway outside the family sleeping quarters. He checked the main entrance to the private wing, making certain access to the suite of rooms was barred from within.

Salinger entered Martin's suite and quietly made his way to the canopied bed. The structure was unoccupied.

"You were always a lucky bastard," he spat, clenching his fist in frustration.

Salinger retreated to the hallway and began to edge toward his parents' room.

When he reached the ornate four poster bed, Salinger forcefully pressed his father's forehead into the pillow. Simultaneously, he jammed the barrel of the Glock into the professor's neck below the jaw. George Salinger opened his eyes to find Jack leering down at him. The professor clutched at Jack's arms, but then relaxed his grip and let both of his arms fall limply onto the mattress.

"We both know the room is soundproofed, Father, but if you utter a single word, I'll blow your head off. Now, get out of bed!"

Nora Salinger had awakened. With a gasp she pressed the back of her hand tightly to her mouth and scooted into a sitting position against the headboard.

"Jack," she cried out, "don't shoot him, I beg of you."

Salinger was embittered to find his mother more concerned about George Salinger's welfare than surprised that Salinger himself was still alive.

"Where is Martin?" Salinger demanded, directing the question to Nora.

"Why, he's not here, Jack," his mother managed.

Salinger kept the barrel of the Glock pressed to George Salinger's neck. Cautiously following Jack's instruction, the professor rose awkwardly to a sitting and then a standing position. Salinger forced the older man to stumble clumsily toward a round table in the center of the room.

"Sit down, Father," he said.

Salinger slowly backed away from the older man, keeping the weapon pointed at his father's head. Jack gestured with the barrel of the gun. George Salinger reluctantly sat down in a high-backed chair.

"You'll never get away with this," the professor growled.

"Is that sweat on your forehead, Father?" Salinger taunted, as he pulled up another chair and sat confronting the professor. He was enjoying the discomfort on his father's face, despite the efforts the older man was making to conceal his anxiety.

"You haven't got the guts to pull that trigger," George Salinger sneered.

"Oh, but you're wrong, Father. I learned a great deal about myself during the excursion to the streets someone arranged for me. Was it your friend, Striker?"

"Striker sent you to the streets at my suggestion, Jack. I never thought you'd survive. I wanted you dead then, and I'm going to enjoy seeing you dead in the very near future."

The remark stung, but Salinger said nothing.

"George," Nora Salinger cried out, "what are you saying?"

"Look at him, Nora, this son of yours. Once again, he's sullied the Salinger name. I can't stand the sight of him!"

Salinger tried to focus through the red film of rage obscuring his vision.

"I killed four men in cold blood several weeks ago, Father," he said. "I think that finally entitles me to the Salinger name."

"You'll never be a Salinger!" the professor said bluntly.

Despite his efforts to contain himself, Salinger's voice broke momentarily.

"Why, Father? Why have you always hated me?"

"Because you're not my son!" the professor shouted, glaring into the barrel of Jack's Glock with haughty arrogance.

"George, please," Nora Salinger cried from the bed, "you don't have to do this."

Salinger slumped back into his chair. The barrel of the firearm slowly descended until the Glock was hanging limply in his hand.

"What are you talking about?" he said, his voice faltering.

"I was to blame," the professor said, his voice subdued. He sat looking at his hands, the display of humility uncharacteristic of him. "I was busy. I was away for long periods of time. We had a stable master in those days. He would take your mother riding. Well...you can guess what eventually happened."

"Is this true, Mother?" Salinger demanded.

Nora Salinger's flushed face answered for her. She raised her eyes and looked at Jack imploringly, but she said nothing.

"I've always loved your mother more than anything in this world," George Salinger said. "I returned to the manor after a protracted absence and her condition was obvious. She confessed everything. I managed to forgive her.

"Now, do what you came here to do," he said, looking up at Jack defiantly. "I'm sick of you and this entire affair."

"What happened to my father?" Salinger demanded, looking from one to the other of these people who had suddenly become strangers.

"Why don't you ask your mother?" George Salinger said.

"Jack, please forgive me," Nora Salinger stammered. "I tried to make certain arrangements," she said with hesitation.

"Is my real father still alive?"

"I don't know, Jack," Nora said honestly. "He was a proud man. He refused any assistance from me. We…I lost track of him many years ago, after Second Independence Day."

Salinger was dumbfounded. He sat slumped in his chair, shaking his head in disbelief.

"Can you possibly understand the pain you might have spared me by telling me about this, Mother. I could have lived my life without trying to measure up to the expectations of this…this animal."

"Please, Jack," his mother pleaded, "don't hurt him. I love him more than you could possibly imagine."

Salinger tried to force down his bitterness.

"Well," he said, "since we've opened the family's secrets, we should address another issue. "Martin is sterile. Now that Charlotte has left him, your son, Professor, will never give you an heir."

"Oh, Jack, then you haven't heard about Charlotte," Nora Salinger said.

"What do you mean, Mother?"

"Charlotte was killed, accidentally, several weeks ago."

For the second time that evening, Salinger was stunned. Guilt seared through him. Could he have done something more for Charlotte?

"Martin was not responsible for any of Charlotte's pregnancies," Salinger said, his voice now caustic. "Your son is sterile…sterile in so many ways. In fact, Charlotte asked me to help her become pregnant. Considering Charlotte's fate, I regret I never had the chance to do that for her."

"We know all about Martin and Charlotte," Jack's mother said, her voice almost inaudible.

"The stupid girl kept a very detailed journal," George Salinger added with sarcasm. "Martin found it."

"But you're wrong about Martin, Jack," Nora Salinger said. He and Marla are together now. Marla is with child…with Martin's son."

"You let Martin murder Charlotte?" Salinger shouted at George Salinger.

"Murdered? Charlotte died accidentally, Jack," Nora Salinger insisted.

"No, Mother, no one ever dies accidentally at Haworth Manor." Turning to the professor, Salinger added with cutting sarcasm. "Perhaps I should enlighten my mother about your hunting expeditions."

"Please, Jack," his mother pleaded, "I can't take anymore of this."

"I have one more revelation to make, Mother. Marla was at peak fertility when I came home for my birthday celebration. We had sex that weekend. Given Martin's deficiency, I'm afraid Marla is carrying my son, not Martin's. And I know, Professor, that you will· ask your friend Striker to retrieve Martin's medical records. When you do, you will confirm his sterility and my paternity will be established.

"Now let's look at your options, Professor. After you confirm my allegations, you could confront Martin. He would be outraged and would probably kill Marla and the child. But you need an heir, Professor, you need *my* son desperately. Without him, your precious estate and the despicable Salinger name will be lost. So you won't tell Martin. I suspect you will arrange the necessary DNA testing to convince Martin that Marla's child is his own.

"Then, of course, you also love Martin, Professor. He is, after all, your only son. You would not want Martin to suffer the pain of knowing he was raising another man's child, the pain I have caused you all of my life.

"And so you will raise my son as if he were Martin's heir. You may even manage to accept him as your grandson, Professor. But you will always know—until the day you die—that not one drop of his blood is your own.

"As for me, I will have to live with the pain of knowing Martin Salinger will raise my child. At least Martin will make the boy physically strong. And you, Mother— and Marla—will make him a human being, a far better man than me.

"One day, he will learn about his real father. I suspect Marla will tell him. And when the time is appropriate, I'll come back for him and take him from you.

"So you needn't worry, Mother. I don't intend to take your precious husband or your first-born son from you. Unfortunately, my son will need them both."

Salinger rose from his seat.

"You'll never escape," George Salinger said. "Striker will hunt you down like a dog and we'll hang your body in the trees to feed the birds. We will hang you next to Dobson."

"Alfred Dobson? Was he another Haworth Manor accident?" Salinger taunted. "Don't waste your time," he added. "By the time the staff find you in the morning, I will be out of your reach. Now go back to the bed, Professor, and lie down with your face in the pillow."

Salinger bound the hands and feet of the professor and then those of his mother.

"I'm sorry, Mother, I know this will be uncomfortable for you."

"You know I have always loved you, Jack," his mother insisted. "You do know that?"

Salinger looked at the pleading expression on Nora Salinger's face. Then he turned and walked away.

"I believe you tried to love me, Mother," Salinger said, pausing at the door of the suite. "I believe you sincerely tried to love me."

CHAPTER 41

▼

Kurt Striker rose from his chair and walked to the window of his office in the Department of Homeland Security. On the Tarmac outside, flight crews were arming a large contingent of Apache helicopters, preparing the aircraft for battle.

"The issue, you see, has always been quite simple. How far could we afford to permit Mrs. Lee-Weston to proceed with her madness?" he said, watching the preparations on the airstrip with fascination.

"Her interest in the psychiatrists was intriguing in the beginning. I really had no idea what she had in mind, until the connection with liberal agitation became apparent, as in the case of our friend Salinger and the others. I have to give her a good deal of credit. Her *Certification of America* has certainly had the propaganda value she anticipated. I admire her originality. The creation of the document—strange as it is in many respects—was a stroke of political genius.

"We could have aborted her operation at any time, of course, but timing is always the most important issue in conducting matters like this. I want you to understand my strategy, in case something unforeseen should happen."

Striker walked back to his desk and sat down.

"Who knows, Colonel, you may have to bring the final phases of our operation to completion on your own.

"President Lee-Weston will have to be disposed of. That much is clear," Striker continued. "The question is, when to effect her demise. Let's look at our options, shall we?

"We could have assassinated the president some time ago, once we had sufficient hard evidence to satisfy the purists on the council of her irrefutable guilt.

Our department would have been cited for patriotic service to the state, and everything would have gone on as before.

"But the consolidation of power requires a great deal of forethought, my young friend. I realized early on that a far better strategy was to allow the president's rebellion to proceed, to a point. With each step Madam Lee-Weston has taken, our revered ministers have become increasingly fearful for their own safety. As you have seen, the Council of Twelve has graciously increased the authority of our department at every juncture.

"The time has arrived, however, to bring the president's little game to a conclusion. We would not want any additional adversity to befall our esteemed ministers…not yet at any rate.

"President Lee-Weston wanted to create a symbol that would spur political dissension in these United States. As the martyred leader of her failed coup, she will become such a symbol herself. Further civil unrest in the name of the martyred president and her co-conspirators is inevitable, as the citizenry continues to pursue her fatuous dream.

"We will allow the discord to proceed apace in the crucial weeks ahead. The Council of Twelve will be forced to delegate even more authority to our department, as the level of agitation escalates. Eventually, we will have to terminate the ministers ourselves, of course. When our consolidated power becomes sufficient, we will effect a coup of our own."

Striker's protégé smiled at him from across the desk.

"I assume interference by the Canadians and the British has been averted, Commander Striker?"

Striker laughed heartily.

"Now, that was a masterstroke on President Lee-Weston's part, Colonel. Harold Weston worked tirelessly to enlist the British. Since her husband's unfortunate accident, the president has also been obsessed with consolidating a British connection.

"No, not to worry, Colonel. When we locked onto Toronto and London from space and informed the British and the Canadians about the vipers in their respective nests, the president's fortunes—as yet unknown to her—collapsed like a house of cards. The element of a surprise attack against our military establishments was the final trump card Mrs. Lee-Weston had. Were it not for your efforts on our behalf, Colonel, she might have pulled it off.

"But once the British and the Canadians learned the price they would pay if any of their people assisted Mrs. Lee-Weston, they turned their respective secret services loose. Most of the dissidents have already been rounded up. But, of course, we will put a stop to Mrs. Lee-Weston long before she learns her foreign support has evaporated.

"But don't you find human nature fascinating, Colonel? Miranda Lee-Weston was naïve enough to believe she would not be betrayed. I find her unyielding trust in the dignity of human nature the most intriguing aspect of the woman's character. The fact that only two of her 56 signatories were disloyal is even more amazing.

"Without the help of our informers, we may never have learned of the president's latent resources. Your role in convincing those individuals to come over to our side has been invaluable, Colonel."

Kurt Striker rose to his feet.

"But you must get on with your work," he said, extending his hand. "Remember, the president must be taken alive. A dead traitor on the battlefield will not be half as useful to us as a martyr we can dispose of as we see fit."

Colonel Cantrell unconsciously smoothed her closefitting flight suit, as she too rose and then shook Commander Striker's hand. She saluted sharply, about faced, and walked out of the room.

Kurt Striker appreciated Dominique Cantrell's striking physical attributes, as he watched his young protégé walk out of the office. He was pleased that his dedication to the memory of his wife placed him above the primitive feelings that might have compromised his working relationship with young Cantrell.

Dominique Cantrell was an ambitious and ruthlessly efficient operative. Striker felt very fortunate that he had discovered someone with her talent. He recalled one of his early interviews with his young protégé. He recognized immediately that she had the uncompromising killer instinct necessary to success and survival in a very demanding profession. He had reviewed digital images of her first assignment under his direction with great interest. Striker had discovered a connection between the president and an aide to one of the ministers. Major Cantrell had been remorseless in taking out her target. Cantrell's demeanor had contrasted strikingly with the abject groveling of the aide, who had pleaded ignobly for her privileged life.

Striker had nurtured Cantrell's meteoric career personally. She had quickly moved through the ranks.

The only blemish on the Colonel's record had been Jack Salinger. Cantrell had played the young psychiatrist with great finesse, but she had made no progress in inducing him to betray the president. Salinger's fate was in question at the moment. He may have died in the streets. If not, he would soon join Miranda Lee-Weston as a foolhardy martyr to a lost cause.

CHAPTER 42

▼

Dominique Cantrell left Commander Striker's office and walked energetically through the corridors of the building that housed the Department of Homeland Security. She felt proud of her mentor's confidence in her.

Jack Salinger had almost derailed Dominique Cantrell's career. Her mission the afternoon she had spent with Salinger in the countryside had been clear. Kurt Striker had given Dominique explicit instructions. But Dominique had never anticipated falling in love with Salinger. He had been her assignment in the beginning, nothing more. She had led him on. But then, she had stupidly fallen in love with him, at least briefly. She was still having trouble expunging memories of the idyllic day she and Salinger had spent by the river. How different her experience with Salinger had been compared with the other targets Striker had assigned to her. How different making love with him had been from the casual physical encounters Dominique had experienced with other Angels or, rarely, with those abhorrent, impersonal machines.

Despite such feelings—which she interpreted now as effeminate weakness—Dominique knew she could never again allow primitive emotions, like her temporary infatuation with Salinger, to derail her rise to the top. Dominique had always been willing to use sex to achieve her aims, but Salinger had come dangerously close to breaking her resolve. She would never make such a mistake again.

Dominique had failed in her attempt to recruit Salinger as a double agent that afternoon. Despite her failure, Commander Striker had assigned Dominique to lead the air assault against the rebellion. She would not fail Kurt Striker again.

Like Striker, Dominique Cantrell held Miranda Lee-Weston in disdain. She shared Striker's assessment of the president as weak, naïve and hopelessly idealistic. Mrs. Lee-Weston should have anticipated the superior forces Striker had at his disposal. The president had fatally underestimated her adversaries.

As for Salinger, Dominique hoped he had already been killed. If he had survived Striker's half-hearted effort to eliminate him, Cantrell herself would hunt him down. She needed to see Salinger crushed in order to regain her objectivity and purge herself of any lingering frailty. The memory of herself mewling beneath Salinger like a schoolgirl or a common whore tightened her stomach.

Dominique was relieved that Kurt Striker had never pursued a physical relationship, though she found him extremely attractive. He clearly had the intelligence to succeed in his quest for leadership of the country. His arguments in favor of rule by a single charismatic leader made sense. The implication that she might succeed him was a thrilling prospect, the culmination of Dominique's quest to become one of the most powerful women in American history.

Colonel Cantrell picked up her pace and walked toward the airstrip outside, where a squadron of Apache turbo choppers stood at the ready. Dominique was about to embark on the most important mission of her career.

CHAPTER 43

▼

Dominique Cantrell reached the sleek Apache turbo-chopper she was to fly in the vanguard of the coming attack on the president's base of operations. The aircraft was a lethal killing machine, one of the most advanced in the arsenal of the U.S. Airforce. For this mission, the Apaches were loaded with explosive canisters of Bionex V-9, a state of the art biochemical weapon.

The guard unit snapped to attention at Dominique's approach. Colonel Cantrell's crew was aboard and ready for action. Dominique boarded the chopper and fired up the engine. She barked a command to the pilots of the surrounding aircraft. She revved the main rotor of her ship and lifted the Apache into the sky.

Cantrell and her fleet were soon flying at low altitude in attack mode with engines at full throttle. Airspeed was approaching 400 miles per hour. Colonel Cantrell activated the Apache's stealth defensive shields, making the aircraft undetectable by radar or thermal scanning. Dominique's breasts tingled beneath the firm pressure of the harness that locked her to her seat. The sensation in her belly was erotic in a way she had rarely experienced.

CHAPTER 44

▼

Miranda Lee-Weston was briefing her officer staff on the timetable for the impending attacks on the surviving ministers. Sealed orders were to be released at 0600 the following morning. Suddenly there was a soft thud in the air overhead that caused the walls of the compound to tremble slightly. Within seconds, the president sensed leaden stiffness throughout her body. She tried to move, but found she could not. She was not actually paralyzed. She had simply lost the will to take any action.

The president remained in a strange state of suspended animation for several minutes. The others in the room were similarly immobilized. Then, several figures wearing biohazard suits burst into the room and forcibly dragged Mrs. Lee-Weston and the others outside.

Miranda Lee-Weston was kneeling on the ground with her hands cuffed behind her back. When she was finally able to lift her head she found the area outside the compound brightly lit. Troops wearing biohazard suits were shooting members of the president's forces in the back of the head as they knelt on the ground. The bodies pitched forward into a trench with obscene finality, like dead birds plunging into the sea from some terrible height.

An officer in gas mask and hot suit approached. After checking a biohazard sensor, the individual removed the cumbersome protective gear. Dominique Cantrell stood menacingly above the group kneeling on the ground.

"I see our new weapon has dispersed sufficiently," she said.

Dominique approached the kneeling president. Miranda Lee-Weston did not look up. She continued to stare at the ground resolutely.

"I am Colonel Dominique Cantrell, Mrs. Lee-Weston. In the name of Com-mander Kurt Striker, of the Department of Homeland Security, I arrest you for high treason against the government of the United States of America."

Dominique snapped her fingers. A subordinate ran up and saluted smartly. "Take these people away," she said.

CHAPTER 45

▼

Salinger was sitting at a bare table across from Adam Kennedy. The sparsely furnished room was located in the latest of the half dozen safe houses the strike force had used since the missile attacks.

Salinger was concentrating on the label of the half-empty bottle of Irish whiskey he was holding in his hand.

"You didn't know Quinlan's children would be aboard the chopper?" Salinger challenged, looking at Kennedy intently.

Adam Kennedy's eyes were fixed on Salinger.

"Get it together, Jack," he said. "Of course we didn't know."

"So one just has to get used to collateral damage, is that it? In guerilla warfare?"

"Unfortunately," Kennedy said, grabbing the bottle from Salinger. He leaned his head back and swallowed hard.

There was a loud knock at the door.

"Yeah?" Kennedy said.

Allen Morrison, the squad communications specialist, opened the door and slumped against the side frame.

"The president has been taken," he said.

Details trickled in throughout the afternoon. The group at the safe house monitored developments on the squad's wireless desktop computer. The National News Service was reporting that Mrs. Lee-Weston had been taken alive. She was being held at Black Ridge Federal Prison, a maximum-security facility.

Kennedy and the others watched somberly as the network conducted a virtual tour of the stockade. Black Ridge was obviously impregnable. The penitentiary had been carved out of solid rock on an island located in the middle of a small lake. Heavily armed blockhouses guarded the entire perimeter. Radar swept the water and airspace for intrusion. At night, the sky above the prison was alive with the glaring beams of searchlights.

The Director of the Department of Homeland Security made a terse announcement later that evening.

"Miranda Lee-Weston, former President of the United States, was tried in absentia several weeks ago," Striker said without emotion. "She has been found guilty of high treason. Sentence—as prescribed by law—will be carried out at noon, EST, on July 4th. The execution will be broadcast nationwide from the Federal Judicial Coliseum at Raven Hill."

The level of frustration in the safe house reached critical mass that evening.

Adam Kennedy had been sitting for hours before a laptop, peering at the topographical holograph of the terrain surrounding Black Ridge Prison.

"There's not a damn thing we can do," he said, as he rose from his chair and slammed his fist into the wall.

"You know what they're going to do to her," Salinger said.

"Of course I know, Jack! What exactly do you expect me to do about it?"

Adam Kennedy picked up the empty whiskey bottle and hurled it into a corner. He stormed out of the room as the splinters scurried across the floor.

CHAPTER 46

▼

Jack Salinger lay sweating and restless on his bunk that night. When sleep did come in small snatches, he was tormented by visions of what was to take place on the 25th anniversary of Second Independence Day…

Naked except for a loincloth, he was dragged into the coliseum in chains. The lights were blinding. The sound was an intense cacophony of booming music and raucous cheers. Salinger recognized the primitive refrains of the blood chant.

The thundering sound was coming from several tiers of loudspeakers, but no one in the audience was cheering. In some sections of the arena, security forces were prodding people to pay attention to the TelePrompTers, but the earthlings standing rigidly before their seats were silent.

Cameras panning the aisle recorded Salinger's slow march to the ring. He was dragged up a short flight of stairs and then pushed toward one of a series of large poles fixed to the floor of the stage. His body was chained to one of the shafts. He was then pushed to a sitting position, his legs extended on the floor in front of his body. The overhead lights burned into his skull like a merciless tropical sun. He recognized President Lee-Weston immediately. She was naked from the waist up—Liberty leading the people—and similarly chained to one of the uprights.

Salinger scanned the crowd sitting nearest his position. He could clearly see the faces of the earthlings standing in the first few rows. They remained impassive and silent, seemingly oblivious to the chants and cries emanating from the loudspeakers.

Suddenly the raucous noise stopped. Salinger recognized the voice of Kurt Striker, speaking in a somber monotone. The crimes of the prisoners were systematically enumerated.

Salinger peered into the lenses of the cameras recording the event. He tried to imagine his family viewing the proceedings from home. He wondered if his mother or her life mate would be able to watch. He knew his brother's eyes would be glued to the screen.

Kurt Striker stopped speaking. The group of attendants began the rigidly pre-scribed ceremony. As the first stage of the punishment for treason against the state, each of the prisoners was garroted to the point of unconsciousness and then allowed to recover. The protocol mandated three repetitions of the procedure. The consequences, should any of the attendants become too zealous and lose their charge, were severe.

Salinger's body twisted against the chains binding his wrists. His legs flailed helplessly as the intense suffocation became overwhelming, before he momen-tarily lost consciousness. The second strangling was worse, but by the time he had recovered from this second application of the cord to his neck, Salinger realized he was narcotizing himself with endorphins. He was able to embrace the suffoca-tion, the third time the ligature was applied.

Phase two of the protocol was over quickly. An attendant approached and with no warning subjected Salinger to emasculation and castration. He then slashed Salinger's abdomen, spilling his intestines onto the floor between his legs. The sudden shocking appearance of his own squirming entrails caused Salinger to faint momentarily. When he regained consciousness, he could see little at first, because of the sweat that was pouring into his eyes. He tried to make eye contact with his fellow sufferers. Through a haze of perspiration, he could barely make out Miranda Lee-Weston. Her head had slumped forward. Salinger surmised that she, too, had lost consciousness momentarily. She, like Salinger and the others, had also been eviscerated.

The chains binding Salinger's wrists were removed. He had no desire to move or to struggle any longer. A strange apathy had replaced any will to resist. He was aware of what would come next. Like the others, he sat passively on the floor, waiting as his abdomen was wrapped with a cloth binding.

Salinger strained to focus on the faces of the earthlings in the first few rows of the audience. The men and women standing before him were now chanting, but the words they were speaking were not those of the blood chant blasting from the surrounding speakers. Salinger strained to read the lips of the man standing clos-est to him. He could not interpret what the man was intoning at first, but sud-denly he realized that this earthling and the others near him were slowly chanting the president's name.

Salinger scanned as many faces as he could before the attendants came for him. Several of the men and women were holding the small cards on which *The Certification of America* had been printed. Those cards bore Jack Salinger's signature.

When his turn came, he was jerked to his feet by two of the attendants and dragged to the block for the final ordeal prescribed by the state. As he was led toward the waiting executioner, he passed Miranda Lee-Weston. She managed to look up at him. He could read compassion and sadness in her face, but no inkling of regret.

Salinger realized that his severed head and quartered body would be displayed to the people to serve as a warning against treason and betrayal of the state. But he would also become a martyr—a modern Nathan Hale who would die for democracy and freedom. His head was forced onto the block…

Salinger bolted awake and sat up in his bed. His body was drenched with sweat. He lurched down the hall to the latrine. Gripping the rim of the seat, he retched into the slowly rising stench. He returned to his room. Sitting with his knees pulled tightly to his chest, he waited for dawn to break in the northeast.

CHAPTER 47

▼

Adam Kennedy looked up at Salinger's haggard face as Jack walked into the conference room in the morning and slumped into a chair.

"You look like shit, Jack," he said.

"We have to do something, Adam."

"Do what? Do exactly what, Jack?" Kennedy said, striking the empty space before him with clenched fists.

"I want to make an attempt at the coliseum."

Kennedy tried to scrape the frustration from his brain by raking his skull vigorously with his fingernails. He stopped the futile massage and placed both palms on the surface of the table. He leaned toward Salinger.

"There is nothing you can do," he said, enunciating each word with cutting deliberation.

"Give me two choppers with stealth shields. I'll get you twelve additional volunteers by nightfall," Salinger said.

"Suicide, Jack…you're asking me to authorize over a dozen…"

"We can't let them mutilate her," Salinger interrupted, slamming his fist onto to the table. "She changed my life, Adam," he said more softly, after a pause. "I have to try something…anything. But I can't let them humiliate her, even if I have to end her life myself."

"Look, Jack, I know how you feel," Kennedy commiserated. "We all feel the same. But I can't let you destroy thirteen people and two valuable aircraft attempting a cockeyed suicidal mission with absolutely no chance of success."

Salinger activated Adam's laptop. He drew a crude plan in virtual space.

"You'll have to use a ground unit to set off some diversionary fireworks as we come in just before noon," Salinger said. "Like you say, the effort would be suicidal. The security forces on the ground wouldn't expect us to try anything so stupid. As you've been telling me for weeks, Adam, in guerilla warfare the element of surprise is always the trump card. If we can't extract her, at least we might be able to save her the indignity of public mutilation."

"You were always crazy, Salinger. Hopelessly romantic...and totally crazy."

"I'm going to bring you a dozen volunteers before the day is out, Adam. Start working on the logistical details. We don't have much time."

Adam Kennedy sat back in his chair.

"I'll think about it," he said. "But I'm not making any promises."

CHAPTER 48

▼

Eight men and five women would make the attempt on July 4th, 2101, the 25th anniversary of Second Independence Day. Adam Kennedy, though remaining skeptical, threw all of his energy into the mission. In the few days available for training, the squad melded into a tightly knit strike force.

The pilots and Salinger had been former Angels. The rest of the crew had once been known as earthlings.

Carrie Hamilton, pilot of the primary chopper, was 26 years old. Len Ross, the pilot of the backup unit was 27. The others were in their late teens or early twenties. Salinger, the only 30 year-old, was known affectionately, as the "old man."

The plan was reviewed endlessly. The choppers would have to penetrate the two-mile wide no fly zone surrounding the coliseum and come in barely off the ground to avoid an expected barrage of surface-to-air missiles. Hamilton and Ross would have no margin for error.

The diversionary barrage was key to any success the teams could hope for. The attack would begin five minutes before touchdown. Several ground units would lob mortars into the coliseum walls on the opposite side of the building from the landing sites. Movement of ground security forces in response to the diversion would hopefully dilute enemy strength on the critical deployment side of the building. In the ensuing confusion, the choppers would land as close to the coliseum as possible. Rick Klinger, the munitions specialist, would blow the targeted entrance while the rest of the personnel provided cover for Salinger, John Lacey, and Sarah Dalton, who would attempt interior penetration.

Adam Kennedy estimated the overall chance of a successful extraction of the president and safe return of both aircraft at far less than one in two hundred. He felt there might be a fifty-fifty chance of entering the coliseum and a one-in-ten chance of preventing what everyone involved called the unthinkable.

Adam Kennedy shook the hand of each of the thirteen participants. The crew slammed helmets and screamed at one another with the mad shrieks of people hoping to divest themselves of all traces of humanity. They knew they had to convince themselves that brute animal strength would allow them to prevail. From the moment the two aircraft lifted off, the mission quickly became surreal.

Salinger, with cold clinical detachment, realized anxiety had narcotized his crew.

The screaming whine of the engine and the grating whop of the rotor blades fed Salinger's fantasy that he was flinging himself and the others straight into the abyss, into the midst of some hellish nightmare.

The flight to the target seemed over before it began.

Carrie Hamilton's throat was constricted as the imposing shadow of the coliseum loomed up before the speeding aircraft. She could see a huge plume of smoke rising in the distance that happily confirmed the successful diversion effected by the collaborating ground forces.

So far, neither chopper had taken a hit from the heavy ordnance bombardment coming from several ground batteries, but the aircraft were now within machine gun range.

Carrie Hamilton had been an avid student of the American Civil War. She thought about the magnificent charge Pickett's confederates had made on the third day at Gettysburg. Many of the Union forces watching the oncoming wall of rebels had described the surging thrust of the doomed confederates as something otherworldly and beautiful.

Carrie glanced over her shoulder at Salinger and her other compatriots in the back of the chopper. She was sure the emotion she was reading on those close-set faces mirrored her own intense feelings. Then she turned back to lock on the approaching coliseum. Machine gun fire began to sweep toward the oncoming aircraft. Carrie could see the flashes from the gun muzzles, flashes of intense light that preceded the barrage of angry missiles coming for them.

At that moment, Carrie was convinced the assault would fail. One or maybe both of the choppers might manage to land, but if they made it that far they would all suffer the same bloody repulse that had cut down the charging confederates at Gettysburg. Neither assault team would be able to rescue President Lee-Weston or reach her in time to carry out a coup de grace.

In Carrie Hamilton's imagination, the projectile that would take her life seemed to be coming for her in slow motion from somewhere ahead. She hoped some great poet would record the events that had happened this day, the last 4th of July of her life. As in the case of the honored dead at Gettysburg, Carrie Hamilton hoped someone, somewhere, would remember she had given her life fighting for freedom.

But then they were on the ground. Salinger and the others had deplaned and were running toward the coliseum. Carrie tried to wipe away the sweat pouring into her eyes. She watched Rick Klinger drop to his knees, raise a rocket launcher to his shoulders, and place a dead-on shot into the heavily bolted entrance corridor nearest them. She watched the projectile twisting like a wounded snake until the side of the building exploded in fire, falling bricks, and debris. She watched Jack Salinger and the others disappear into a cloud of smoke and flame.

Machine gun hits were pinging across the concrete. The merciless pops seemed to be edging in Carrie's direction like swarms of maddened wasps furious at not finding an immediate victim. To her left she watched one of the crew of the backup chopper take a hit to the neck. She watched the arms reach up slowly, fail to reach the place of torment, and then fall limply to the sides as the woman's body pitched forward to the ground. Time slowed to an agonizing crawl. The whine of the engine was like a drill bit boring into her brain. Carrie Hamilton sat shaking and sick in the cockpit waiting for death.

The explosions had precipitated the first inklings of panic inside the coliseum. Most of those in the crowd were screaming uncontrollably. Salinger's body seemed to be moving agonizing slowly down the sloping aisle toward the center of the arena. He seemed to be floating through space, even though he knew he was running at full speed with every ounce of strength he had left.

He rushed toward the stage. To his side he thought he saw gunfire, but he could do nothing but wait for the murderous projectiles to rip through his flesh. To his left, he could hear Sarah Dalton's labored breathing. The sound was harsh, like the raspy cry of the wide-open valve of a fully stoked steam engine. He wanted to stop, to comfort Sarah, to beg her to forgive him, but all he could do was hurl his body forward and drive his protesting muscles far beyond the threshold of pain.

An armed guard stepped into the aisle and raised a machine gun. Before Salinger could think of responding his ear was shattered by several sharp cracks that seemed to explode inside his head. Dalton had taken the guard out, shooting from the hip without hesitation.

They reached the stage. Salinger recognized Miranda Lee-Weston. But then the unthinkable happened. As he was running toward her, one of the state executioners shot the president in the chest at point-blank range.

Salinger would never forget the cry of protest that bellowed out of his lungs. He put round after round into the president's assassin until Dalton wrenched at his arm and ordered him to stop firing. They had reached the president seconds too late to save her life. John Lacey rushed up on Salinger's right and began to release Mrs. Lee-Weston's bindings.

Salinger dropped to his knees before the president's slumping body. At least they had accomplished something. At least Miranda Lee-Weston would suffer no further indignity.

CHAPTER 49

▼

Kneeling at her side, Salinger could not take his eyes off the president's face. He owed everything to this remarkable woman; she had changed his life, but he had failed to save hers. He was aware of increasing small arms fire coming from various locations inside the building. He expected to be hit at any moment. He wanted to destroy the television cameras obscenely panning the stage and recording this terrible event.

Salinger glanced to the side and was shocked to find that the front of Sarah Dalton's pullover was bright crimson. Had her body-armor been penetrated? Sarah was clutching at her chest. Salinger was certain she had been hit. As he twisted toward Dalton, intent on staunching the flow of blood, Sarah extracted a scarlet object from her blouse.

Salinger glanced over his shoulder. He tried to convince himself that he was alive, that he was not dreaming. Security guards were being shot or beaten by surging groups of former earthlings. The crowd was turning on the government forces in the arena.

Sarah had unfolded a large piece of fabric and had spread the cloth onto the floor of the stage. Salinger could not believe his eyes. Dalton was unfolding a primitive hand sewn flag—a rendering of the old Stars and Stripes. Over Salinger's shoulder, the reddish eye of a camera zoomed in like a predatory insect on the original American flag.

"Where did you get this?" Salinger stammered.

"I've been working on it for days," Dalton said. "I wanted them to find the flag on my body; I was hoping they might bury me..." she said. "Help me wrap Miranda in the standard, Jack."

As Salinger and Dalton were struggling with the flag, he noticed a security guard to his right taking careful aim at them. He reached for the Glock but, before he could get off a shot, the guard's face exploded. The shooter saluted and then moved off in search of another target.

Carrie Hamilton sat rocking in the cockpit with her eyes tightly closed. Her knuckles were white as she gripped the stick.

"Come on, people...Come on!"

Carrie opened her eyes and tried to look out beyond the billowing smoke that was obscuring her vision. She would have traded anything for the soft warm darkness of a good latrine.

Several hundred men and women, some carrying shovels, picks, or axes, had surged over the barricades surrounding the coliseum and were now running toward the two choppers. To her right, Hamilton could see a group of government troops carrying a rocket launcher moving toward her position. The squad halted and began to set up their field ordnance less than a hundred yards away. In the distance, Carrie could make out an armored vehicle slowly moving into view. She knew she had no chance to withstand this new onslaught. Her survival instincts were screaming into the back of her brain that the mission was doomed and that she should lift off to fight another day.

The crowd of insurgents seemed to be reading her imminent danger. A large group veered toward the rocket launcher detachment. Government troops began to pick off the unarmed rebels as they came on. Suddenly, the trooper kneeling in firing position with the rocket launcher pitched forward onto the concrete. Carrie Hamilton gasped. One of the troops in the detachment had been the shooter. This individual picked up the rocket launcher, turned the weapon on the approaching armored vehicle, and fired. The lumbering personnel carrier disintegrated in a massive ball of flame. A dense cloud of acrid black smoke drifted toward the entrance of the coliseum.

Hamilton could hear nothing above the roar of the chopper's engine, but the gesticulations of the crowd of insurgents convinced her that an immense roar was filling the air.

Then she saw them. Dalton, Lacey, and Salinger emerged from the wall of smoke. Lacey had been hit and was limping badly. He and Dalton were helping Salinger, who was carrying something in his arms wrapped in what? The splotches of red, white, and blue coalesced in Carrie's memory. She recognized the configuration of outlawed original American flag.

"Oh, my God," Hamilton cried out, when she realized the significance of what she was witnessing. The president had been hit. Perhaps they'd lost her.

Intense small arms fire was coming from the starboard side of the chopper. The swelling crowd of rebels had picked up weapons. Troops loyal to the government were being given no quarter in the ensuing firefights.

Hamilton could now make out the strain on Salinger's face. The muscles of his neck were taut, standing out like iron bars as he struggled toward the chopper. But then the crowd of insurgents came to a halt. The crowd parted before Salinger and the others. The collective spirit of the growing crowd seemed to sense what had happened in the coliseum. People—including increasing numbers of government troops—stopped in their tracks. Some began to kneel as the president's body passed. Others snapped to attention and smartly saluted the blood stained Stars and Stripes.

As the flag-draped body of the president moved past the windshield of the helicopter, Carrie Hamilton felt reality fragmenting like a fading holograph. She began to gasp uncontrollably, drawing violent breaths deeply into her chest. Then she was jolted back into the scene. She sensed the aircraft settle with the added weight astern, as the surviving crew boarded.

A violent explosion suddenly rocked the interior of the coliseum. Blocks of concrete fell from the roof and a wall of fire and smoke emerged through the roof.

Carrie Hamilton glanced over at Len Ross in the back-up chopper. Her eyes misted with complex emotions, she gave Ross a thumbs-up. The two Apaches slowly lifted off. Passing through the cover of dense smoke and vapor emerging from the coliseum, the choppers banked sharply to starboard and then roared off toward the horizon.

CHAPTER 50

▼

Five members of the combined assault force had been killed at the coliseum. John Lacey's wounds also proved fatal; he died four days after the choppers had returned to base.

The Department of Homeland Security clamped down hard on the rebel forces following the death of Mrs. Lee-Weston. When the National News Service broadcast the collapse of anticipated support from England and Canada, the heart was taken out of the uprising. Twenty-four of the signatories to Miranda Lee-Weston's *Certification of America* were hunted down and later executed on national television.

Military tribunals summarily shot any of the defecting troops who had been members of the officer class. Those who eluded capture disappeared into the underground, where they joined guerilla units under the overall command of Adam Kennedy.

Thirty days following the death of President Lee-Weston, the entire Council of Twelve was wiped out in a coordinated series of ruthless assassinations. Members of the Council's administrative staff, including Professor George Salinger, were placed under house arrest. Kurt Striker, former director of the Department of Homeland Security effected a bloody coup that placed him in power as the first absolute dictator to rule the *citizens* of the United States of America. One of Striker's initial actions—the first of a series of increasingly popular reforms—was to abolish the designations, Angel and earthling.

Jack Salinger watched the ceremony in celebration of Kurt Striker's rise to absolute political power. He could not take his eyes from Dominique Cantrell, who was standing proudly at the new leader's side.

The president's body had been flown to the remote mountain redoubt that had been Adam Kennedy's headquarters prior to the uprising.

At a quiet graveside ceremony, Miranda Lee-Weston was buried in an unmarked tomb. As had been done to preserve the inviolability of the burial chamber of Abraham Lincoln in Springfield, the president's sarcophagus was interred encased in solid concrete.

Adam Kennedy addressed the assembled forces that somber day.

"Someday this place will become a national shrine, comparable to the burial site of John Fitzgerald Kennedy—the great memorial our country lost with the destruction of Arlington, Virginia. We have all read of the perpetual flame that was designed to burn there forever. We have all read of the intense pain, laced with an overwhelming sense of national pride and patriotism, that Kennedy's memorial produced in every American fortunate enough to have visited that hallowed ground.

"Today, I make this pledge. Someday, a comparable memorial to Miranda Lee-Weston, 62nd President of the United States of America, will be constructed in this place sacred to her memory. I hope we will be the architects of that memorial. If not, those who follow us will complete the task for us. Until that time, those of us who believe in the principles of American democracy and freedom—principles that Miranda Lee-Weston espoused and died for—will defend her resting-place with our lives. An honor guard will perpetually preserve this place from harm.

"And so my friends," Adam Kennedy concluded, pausing to engage Jack Salinger's unwavering eyes, "let us go forward and continue to fight on in Mrs. Lee-Weston's cherished name."

To be continued…

0-595-31498-8